LAST

VICTIM

An absolutely gripping crime mystery with a massive twist

HELEN H. DURRANT

Detective Rachel King Thrillers Book 5

Joffe Books, London
www.joffebooks.com

First published in Great Britain in 2021

This paperback edition was first published
in Great Britain in 2022

ISBN: 978-1-80405-203-7

PROLOGUE

People are far too trusting. Take the couple tonight. Lee's tempted to warn them, remind them that they know nothing about her, a total stranger. But she says nothing. Instead, she just smiles and nods, looks at the precious bundle they've left in her care and assures them it'll all be fine.

But that's a lie.

They leave. She gives it thirty minutes and then makes her move. There is work to do. Lee takes off the agency tabard Ronzo gave her and changes into her own dark clothing that she'd brought with her in her bag. No need for the pretence anymore.

She prepares the infant, takes him from his cot, puts a blanket over him and places him in the car seat. A short whine of protest but he's soon sleeping peacefully again. Time to go. Carrying him with care, Lee makes for the front door of the apartment. She takes the lift down to the ground floor and walks out of the main entrance. There's CCTV but she's got the hood of her top pulled low over her face and she's confident the police won't retrieve any useful images. Parked several metres away, a silver car waits in the shadows. The driver — Ronzo — flashes the headlights once. He's spotted her.

1

"Any trouble?"

"No." She leans over and gently sets down the car seat behind him. The infant doesn't wake.

"You've been careful?" he asks. "Done as I said, not left anything traceable behind, like a used cup in the sink?"

"I'm not an idiot. You don't need to tell me what to do, this is my gig."

"You're wrong, Lee. We do what the boss tells us. She's the one giving out the instructions and paying us for our services."

Lee gives him a hard stare. "I told you at the beginning, I work only for myself. You'd do well not to forget it."

The infant gives a funny little squeal. Waking up, time to go.

"I'm done," she says, peeling off her gloves.

He passes her a roll of notes. "We've been well paid for this, here's your share."

"What'll happen to him?"

Ronzo gives her a wicked smile. "Who knows? That's up to the boss, and I can't guarantee it'll be good." He laughs.

Not her concern. She's got what she wanted, it's just a pity she won't be privy to the horror this will cause his parents. Lee throws the tabard and ID badge at him, stuffs the notes into her pocket and walks off without so much as a backward glance. Shame about the baby, but it's best not to think about that. Time to concentrate on the positives. Tonight, Lee got a measure of revenge on the infant's murdering father. She'd also sorted a problem. She now has money for food, booze and a little to put by for the next phase.

CHAPTER ONE

Day One: Sunday

The call came just as Detective Chief Inspector Rachel King was emerging from the shower. Dripping wet and struggling to keep her towel from falling, she grabbed the mobile, saw the caller's name and swore under her breath.

"This had better be good, Elwyn. It's almost midnight on a Sunday and I'm not officially back until the morning," she snapped.

"Sorry, Rachel, I wouldn't have rung, but Kenton insisted."

Kenton. Superintendent Mark Kenton to give him his full title. Her boss. She should have known. He'd been itching to get her back from maternity leave for weeks now.

Rachel sighed. "Isn't there anyone else?"

"We're really pushed at the station. DCI Baxter's team are working on the robberies in Ardwick, otherwise it would have been him."

"Okay, what is it?"

"We've got a missing child. He was left with a babysitter and taken from the family home while the parents were out. There's no trace of either the child or the sitter."

"You're presuming the sitter is responsible?"

"It looks that way," Elwyn said. "There's been no ransom demand so far. I can't make headway with the mother. She's hysterical. She's crying so much she can barely speak."

"Do they know the sitter?" Rachel asked.

"No, but the girl came from an agency they've used before. But there is something else." He fell silent for a moment. "The baby's father is Scott Agnew."

That knocked the wind out of her. Agnew was trouble, allegedly a member of a Manchester organised crime gang called the Trio. They were suspected of being into large scale drug distribution and money laundering. The story was that over the last few years the Trio had got rid of the opposition and now ruled supreme in the city. They were ruthless and had friends in high places. Not people you wanted to mess with. The police had picked up various minor associates for dealing and other misdemeanours, but up to now, no one had been prepared to give evidence against those at the top. "You suspect this is down to someone with a score to settle, or who might be attempting a takeover?"

"Both are high on the list of possibilities, Rachel — you know Agnew's reputation. Given that Jed is out of the frame, it was inevitable that someone would rise to the top. But unfortunately, we've not just got Agnew, we've got the three of them — Agnew, Ray Hutton and Brendan Blackmore. Not that we've ever been able to pin much on any of them."

Same story as with Jed McAteer, although he had redeemed himself of late by helping the police. "Regardless of who the father is, our priority has to be the infant. No ransom demand, you said?" Rachel asked.

"Not yet."

"The mother?"

"As I said, distraught. I've tried everything but I can't get a word out of her. You're a new mum, maybe your shared experience could help get her talking."

"Has the husband said anything?" she asked.

"No, and he's been far too quiet for my liking. I suspect he knows something. He's comforting his wife but won't say who might have done this, despite being asked. He must have his suspicions. Given that it's his son that's missing I'd have expected him to drop a name or two."

"He might be telling the truth."

Elwyn sighed. "The atmosphere in their home is so emotionally charged I really couldn't say. We need to get the mother talking, and you'll certainly make a better job of it than me. Kenton reckons you can play the empathy card, and I agree."

"Where?"

"An apartment block overlooking New Islington Marina. I'll text you the address," he said.

"Okay, I'll be there as soon as I can."

Elwyn was right to ring her, she couldn't ignore something like this. If this had happened to any of her kids, and particularly her six-month-old baby, Len, she'd want someone like herself on the job too.

She dressed quickly — jeans, a sweater and her favourite black boots. There was no time to fix her hair properly, so she gave it a rub with a towel and scraped it, still limp from the shower, into a ponytail. Since giving birth to Len, she'd lost weight, making her features sharper. What the hell. It was late, and who was going to look at her anyway?

"Going somewhere?" Jed said drowsily. "Only the bed's nice and warm and Len's sleeping for once."

Tempting as that was, she had to go. "Sorry, Jed, this is work, and it's something serious."

"Kenton should know better, you're not due back until the morning."

True, but given her return was only a few hours away, Jed was splitting hairs. "This is what it's like, Jed. This is my work life in the raw. You knew what you were taking on." She smiled. "Anyway, this'll be good practice — your first night on your own with Len." She gave him that *we spoke about this* look and grabbed her jacket. "If I'm not back, make sure Mia gets off to school on time in the morning and that you sort Len. Don't let him stew in a mucky nappy, just get stuck in, and give him his bottle before he screams the place down. And remember he's teething."

"Anything else?"

Rachel made for the door, and then turned and kissed him. "Any serious problems, ring me."

Rachel counted herself a lucky woman. After years of pushing Jed McAteer to the back of her mind and pretending she didn't love him, finally the fates had decreed that they should be together. His criminal past long behind him, he was now one of Manchester's most successful property developers. The name Jed McAteer was once again well known, but not for the wrong reasons. They had their son, Len, a beautiful home Jed had built for the three of them and Rachel's two teenage daughters. The cottage was a happy place, and for the first time in years, Rachel felt content. She had a lot to be grateful for.

* * *

Marina Apartments were new and high spec. The address Elwyn had sent her was on the top floor, with a view over the water and the coming and going of its canal boats.

Elwyn met her in the hallway. "Thanks for doing this, Rachel. We're getting nowhere. The mother's name is Louise, the husband you know. Officially he and his two partners are into property development, a similar business to Jed's. She doesn't work. They went out tonight to have dinner with some friends. When they returned at midnight, both the babysitter and the infant had vanished. They'd used their usual babysitting agency and had been quite happy to leave the baby."

Rachel felt her stomach flip. For a moment she experienced the shock and pain she'd feel if something similar happened to Len. "Where are they?"

"In the sitting room."

She followed him through. The apartment was large with vaulted ceilings, very modern and with minimal furnishing. The décor throughout was in off-white. She nudged

Elwyn. "Couldn't live with this lot. Looks like a show apartment. I like my place comfortable."

The parents were sitting together on a red leather sofa. She recognised Scott Agnew from the newspapers. He had his arm around his weeping wife. He was in his fifties, and his wife looked about thirty years his junior.

"I'm DCI King," Rachel told them. "I'll be heading up the search for your son." Movement from the adjoining room caught her eye. Dr Jude Glover, the senior forensic scientist, was already hard at work. "I see the forensic team are already on it. If your babysitter left any trace at all, they'll find it," she said.

Scott Agnew nodded. "The agency we use is called 'Safe Hands.' It's a day nursery that also offers a child sitting service." He handed her their card. "'Safe Hands.' That's a bloody joke given what's happened. The girl told us she was new, said her name was Kate. She had the identity badge, wore the tabard and seemed to know what she was doing."

"She stole my baby," Louise wailed. "Why would she do that? What will she do with him?"

Agnew held his young wife tighter. Though she'd seen his photo, Rachel had never met him in person before. "What's your son's name and how old is he?" she asked.

"James, and he's two months." Louise stared at Rachel with wide, tear-filled eyes. "He'll be missing me." She turned to her husband and pushed him away. "It's all your fault."

CHAPTER TWO

Rachel let the remark go for the moment. Louise was talking about her husband's criminal activities, had to be, but if she pried to much at this point and he got angry, they'd get nowhere. "We'll do our level best to bring James home," she told Louise gently. "But we'll need your help. Everything you can recall about the sitter for starters."

Scott Agnew answered. "We've used them a number of times, and they've always been sound. We've never had any bother before."

"You said it wasn't your usual sitter — did you query that with the company?"

Louise looked at her. "No, should I have? It didn't occur to me. She had the ID badge around her neck, and as I said, seemed to know what she was doing. We had no reason to call the agency."

"Did you ring home at any time tonight, check in with the sitter?" Rachel asked Louise.

"I did. Remember, Scott, I told you I couldn't get a reply."

That could narrow down the timescale. "You rang the house, and no one picked up? What time was this?" Rachel asked.

"About nine. I wanted to come straight home, but Scott wouldn't hear of it."

He waved this aside. "Tonight was important. A business dinner with a few associates. And it's not as if we're out on the tiles every night. I suppose you think this is all my bloody fault." He was focused on Rachel. "All these stupid questions are wasting precious time. Whatever preconceived ideas you have about me are wrong, and if you allow them to get in the way, I'll have your job." He glared at her. "Now get out there and find my son."

Was this genuine worry talking, or was it just another example of the temper he was famous for? Whichever it was, Rachel needed to take the heat out of the interview. She looked around and spotted a photograph of an infant on a shelf. "Is this James?"

"Yes, we only had it done last week," Louise said.

"May I take it? You'll get it back." Rachel smiled at her.

"I don't want him in the papers," Agnew said at once. "I don't want to turn on the news and see him there either. In fact, the fewer people who know about this, the better."

"If we're to get your son back, we may need the public's help. We need people to come forward, tell us if they've seen him anywhere."

He got to his feet and stared at Rachel, his face close to hers, his eyes blazing. "The only people who need to know about this are us and the investigating team. Joe Public will just muddy the waters. I know how it goes. Let the masses know and you'll have sightings from Cornwall to the north of Scotland."

From the look on his face, Rachel knew he wasn't for changing his mind. They stared at each other for a moment. In his position, she'd move heaven and earth to get her child back. Maybe his reticence had something to do with his criminal activities.

"Are any of his things missing?" Elwyn asked, putting an end to the tension.

"His car seat, a pack of nappies and two feeds ready made up in case. They were in the fridge," Louise said.

Rachel nodded. "Then whoever took him was obviously going to care for him. You can take comfort from that."

That had Louise in tears again. "Depends on who it was." She turned to her husband and laid into him with her fists. "This is down to you! You and your dodgy friends. This is one of them teaching you a lesson. Ask him," she yelled at the detectives. "Make him tell you who took my son. He knows."

Scott Agnew seemed unmoved by her outburst. "She's overwrought, doesn't know what she's saying."

"Oh yes I do. I'm not stupid, you know. This is payback. You've upset someone, Scott, gone too far, and you need to tell the detectives the truth."

Agnew looked up at them. "This has hit Louise hard. I work in property, and my company is currently refurbishing half the buildings in Manchester. It's a cut-throat business, sure. I have rivals, but none of them would pull a stunt like this."

Ignoring him for the moment, Rachel hunkered down in front of Louise. "Mrs Agnew, what you just said about your husband's friends, do you have anyone specific in mind? Someone you know bears a grudge against your family?"

"Ask him," she screamed, waving a fist at her husband. "He cheats and schemes, but this time he's got it wrong and now me and my baby have to pay the price."

Rachel caught Elwyn's eye. They both knew she wasn't talking about property development.

Agnew's face reddened but he kept his voice low. "I'm a businessman, and rivals come with the territory. But there's not a problem, I assure you," he said to Rachel.

"You're sure, Mr Agnew? There is no one in any, er, aspect of your life who would do this?"

He gave her a filthy look by way of a reply, sat down again beside his wife and pulled her close. "What're you insinuating? Stupid police. Always the same. Damned suspicious morons, the lot of you."

Rachel wasn't rising to the bait, arguing with the man would solve nothing.

"We've got the CCTV footage from the two cameras on this road," Elwyn said, "plus the one in the lobby. We're also talking to the neighbours."

"You'll be lucky there," Agnew said. "There's only one other apartment on this floor, they're rarely at home and they don't have any private CCTV."

Ignoring him, Rachel handed Elwyn the photo and then turned her attention back to Louise. "I'll arrange for a female family liaison officer to be with you. It's her job is to keep you informed. You can speak to her about the case, tell her anything you remember."

Louise Agnew nodded.

"Is that really necessary?" Agnew said.

"Yes," Rachel replied. "It's possible you'll shortly receive a ransom demand. We'll monitor your calls — your landline and all your mobiles. An officer from our team will come and set it all up."

Rachel disappeared into the kitchen for a word with Jude. "Got anything useful?"

"No, our kidnapper was far too careful for my liking. Not a print on any of the surfaces, no cups left in the sink, we're still looking but nothing so far."

"Pity. The mother is in bits, which is understandable, but hubby's not being much help."

"You know who he is, don't you?" Jude whispered. "Been around a long time but if there's any prizes going for this year's Manchester villain of the year, he'd win hands down. It's just a shame we can't make anything stick."

"Got something on the go currently, has he?" Rachel asked.

"I hear the odd rumour in my line of work, same as you."

Rachel shook her head. "Not me. I've been out of the loop for a while."

"Well, we had the body of a teenage girl brought in a couple of weeks back, a rough sleeper. A young woman came to the morgue to identify the body, told us she was the dead girl's friend. It hit her hard, she got very upset. She blamed him in there."

"Did she offer any proof?"

"No, she said very little at all and once she knew her friend was well and truly dead, she did one. One minute she's sitting in the waiting room in tears, the next — gone."

"I think Agnew must have upset someone big time, possibly a rival firm and this is his reward. We need to find the infant, Jude. Before the unthinkable happens."

"Talking of infants, how's yours?"

Rachel smiled. "He's doing fine, he's a lot bigger than when you last saw him."

"Why Len?" Jude tipped the contents of the rubbish bin onto a plastic sheet. "Seems an odd name for a baby. These days the fashion seems to be for Callum or Jake and suchlike."

"Jed's dad was called Leonard, so Len it is. Leonard King McAteer." Rachel laughed. "He'll grow into it, and besides, it suits him in a funny sort of way."

"Well there's nothing in here," Jude said, completing her examination of the bin's contents. "Sorry, Rachel, nothing of any help, but we'll keep looking."

"Thanks, Jude."

Rachel went back into the living room. Louise was still weeping, while Scott Agnew paced the floor. "It's late, you should try and get some rest," Rachel told Louise. "Forensics will continue their work for a little longer and the FLO will be here first thing in the morning. If you want to speak to me, here's my card." She handed one over. "We'll be around, speaking to the neighbours and others further down the block."

"Sleep? You must be joking," Agnew said. "I doubt she'll ever sleep again."

* * *

Rachel and Elwyn left the apartment and stood outside in the corridor for a few minutes. She nodded at a door a few metres away. "One other flat on this floor."

The doors to the apartments were both on one side of the corridor. Facing them were floor-to-ceiling windows which gave a spectacular view out over the city.

"Are you the police?"

Rachel turned around to see a boy of about twelve, his face stuck in a telescope which was trained on the night sky.

"Meteor shower," he said simply. "But there's too much light pollution for a proper view."

Rachel smiled at him. "Interesting hobby. But it's a bit late. Do your parents know you're out here?"

He nodded.

Rachel turned back to Elwyn. "Don't know about you, but I'm whacked. A couple of hours' sleep wouldn't go amiss."

"You go," he said. "I'll hang on here, make sure we get everything we need."

"Are you here because of James?" the boy asked.

"Yes," Rachel said.

"That girl took him."

The two detectives stopped talking and turned to look at him. "Did you see her?" Rachel asked.

"Yes," he said. "She was dressed like a boy, but I saw her arrive, so when she left I knew she'd put on other clothes as a disguise. She had James in his car seat."

CHAPTER THREE

Rachel went over to the boy. "You saw her clearly — the girl with James? Did you see if she was with anyone?" If he had, this was the most vital piece of information they had so far.

He nodded. "She didn't see me. I was further up there. She put James into a silver car with a man. He drove away and she ran off."

"What's your name?"

"Andrew."

Rachel smiled at him. "Well, thanks, Andrew, that's really helpful." She looked up and down the corridor, wondering what he was doing out here on his own at this time of night. "Are your parents still up?"

"Not sure."

"I'm going to knock on your door and find out. Meanwhile, perhaps you will tell my colleague here exactly what you saw, so he can write it in his notebook."

"Can't yet. I need to watch the stars."

Rachel was about to reply when a woman came out of the apartment next to the Agnews'.

"Andrew, it's very late. You should be in bed by now." She looked at the detectives, a frown on her face. "Is he bothering you?"

"No, not at all." Rachel showed the woman her badge. "And you are?"

"Andrew's mum."

"James Agnew was kidnapped tonight, and Andrew's just told us he saw who took him."

"Did you?" his mother asked.

He nodded.

"We'd like Andrew to tell us everything he can recall. It might help."

"I can't yet," Andrew called to them. "The meteor shower has started."

The woman looked at her son helplessly and shook her head. "He doesn't mean to be cheeky. It's just that he's so wrapped up in his hobby. Stargazing is all he's done since he was small. He's always found the night sky fascinating. He's so into in his own interests that he can come across as rude."

"We won't take up much of your time," Rachel told the lad.

"It might be better if you speak to him inside," his mother said. "Fewer distractions." She went over to her son and picked up the telescope. "Enough for now, Andrew. These people want a word with you and it's important. You want to help them find James, don't you?"

The lad nodded. He looked at Rachel. "Do you want the registration number of the car the man drove off in? I expect that would help you find him."

Rachel stared at him, amazed. That was quick thinking for a young boy. "You got it? Did you write it down?"

"No need. I remember it." He nodded. "And the girl spat some chewing gum into that bin over there as she left."

"Elwyn, will you get a statement from Andrew along with that registration number? I'll tell Jude about the gum."

* * *

Rachel went back into the Agnews' apartment. The couple were arguing. At this time of night, it was something she could do without.

"He doesn't give a damn about James," Louise said angrily to Rachel. "And why should he? He didn't want him in the first place. Scott's been married before and has other children, he only agreed to have James to keep me quiet."

"You know that's not true," he said. "I love James, really I do."

"No, you don't," she levelled at him. "You're a selfish bastard. You've got no time for anyone but yourself."

Rachel left them to it and went to find Jude, who was in the kitchen, dusting the fridge for prints. "There's a bin along the corridor. The girl who took James spat some chewing gum into it."

Jude looked up and cocked her head to one side. "Someone saw her?"

"Yes, a young lad stargazing at the far end of the corridor. He watched her get into a car outside and even got the registration number."

Jude smiled. "Stroke of luck. I'll retrieve the gum and start tests in the morning. Where's the lad now?"

"Elwyn's getting a statement. That pair in there," she nodded towards where the Agnews were sitting. "Heard anything useful while they've been bickering?"

"Sorry, Rachel, I was too intent on my work. I'll ask the others when we're back at the lab. If there's anything to report, I'll ring you."

CHAPTER FOUR

By the time the two detectives were ready to leave, it was nearly four in the morning. "I'm off home, grab a couple of hours," Rachel said, unlocking her car door. "Expect me in about nine."

Elwyn smiled at her. "It's good to have you back. You've been missed."

"Oh, I'm sure DCI Hennessey was a reasonable replacement."

"She was rarely in. Mother problems, I believe."

Rachel nodded. "The woman has dementia. Poor Nell, it can't be much fun."

"Nell Hennessey wasn't a problem, but that sergeant of hers was another matter. I'm not sorry to lose her," Elwyn said.

"So it's the old team. Suits me," Rachel said.

"There are a few differences," Elwyn said. "Jonny is hell bent on getting a promotion. Amy too in her own way."

Jonny she could understand, he was a good detective, but DC Amy Metcalfe veered between being flaky and reasonably competent. Her resolve to make a go of a career in the police was sound enough, provided she could sort out the laziness.

"There is something you should know," Elwyn said. "There are rumours flying around about our Amy."

Rachel grinned. "Well, we all know what she's like. Something of a man-eater."

"Current gossip has it that she's set her sights on Kenton, and that he's not complaining."

Now this did surprise Rachel. She'd never have put the pair together — there was the age difference for starters. "What d'you think? Kenton can't be serious, surely."

"I think Amy is tired of trying to make it by hard work alone and is using a different tack," he said.

"In that case we'll have to watch her. This gets out, it'll be her job, not Kenton's. The man will have his escape route planned. He won't risk his career for someone like Amy Metcalfe." Rachel climbed into her car. "I'll weigh it up when I'm back in. We'll bring the team up to speed in the morning, and meanwhile Jude will process that gum for DNA. With luck it'll give us a match."

With a wave to Elwyn, she took the main route into the city and then towards the A6. At this early hour traffic was light — she should be home soon and able to get her head down. She was tired but glad to be back doing the job she loved. Hopefully, Jed would soon come to terms with sharing the childcare and they'd get into some sort of routine.

* * *

"He's just not for sleeping." Jed was pacing the sitting room floor, a smiling Len in his arms. "I've fed him, changed him, put him down three times already but the little bugger just yells the place down. He's missing his mummy," Jed said, handing him over. "Are you sure this back to work thing is such a good idea?"

Rachel shot him a look. That subject wasn't up for discussion. Work was where she belonged. Yes, they had Len, but one way or another they'd have to make it work. "I'm off to bed," she said. "Early start."

"Well, I'll have to leave you to it for a while. Phone call from one of my site managers. There's been a spot of trouble."

"Which manager and why does it need you? Can't he cope? I thought that came with the title *Manager*?"

"Getting these properties up and sold is important, Rachel. I can't risk things going wrong." He kissed her cheek. "I won't be long. I'll try and make it back for breakfast but failing that, Len's in nursery tomorrow anyway."

Rachel nodded, too tired to argue the point. Months ago, when she'd first told Jed about the pregnancy, he'd assured her that he'd be there, that he employed people skilled enough to ensure he got all the time off he needed. So much for that. First hint of bother, Rachel's demanding job or not, and he leaves her to it.

CHAPTER FIVE

Day Two: Monday

She was one of the invisible. She'd learned to disappear and was good at it. An entire night could pass and no one gave her a second look.

Sitting in the shadows, she, on the other hand, saw it all. The fighting, the kids dealing dope, the young girls touting their bodies at each car that passed. Didn't they realise just how dangerous life on the street was?

"Lee!" Someone, a man, was shouting at her. "There's sandwiches and hot drinks going at the shelter. Food, Lee. We should go."

She shook her head. She wasn't hungry. She'd bought herself a pizza earlier with some of the money she'd earned last night. "You go, Joe, but be careful. Anyone bothers you, do one quick."

He nodded. "Sure you don't want a sandwich?"

"I'll get something later. I've got other plans."

"Well, don't hang about here too long. I heard the coppers have been nosing around asking questions again. Looking for drugs, I suppose."

She smiled at him. "I'll be fine. No one notices me."

"I'm sure they do," he said, giving her a sideways glance.

"Flatterer. Go and get your food. I'll catch you later."

She watched Joe limp off towards his first bite of the day. Three months back, he'd been set on by a bunch of morons. Prior to that he'd been fast on his feet and fit. Punishment they called it, as they wrecked his life. One mistake, that's all it took. He'd delivered drugs for a dealer and kept some of the money back. The dealer, who worked for Agnew and his crew, had beaten Joe to a pulp. The injuries left Joe with cruel reminders that'd stay with him for the rest of his life — the broken leg, shattered anklebone and the loss of two fingers. Now he couldn't walk properly, never mind run. They'd crippled him, and all for fifty quid.

With Joe out of sight, she got to her feet, stretched, and ran her long, thin fingers through her short blonde hair. She patted both pockets of her jeans. Her mobile was in one and the money she'd earned last night in the other. The cash felt reassuring, it represented a way out for her. Life on the streets was hard, no one had much, and Lee kept her stuff close. Her spare clothing and other essentials were in a backpack that went everywhere with her, except for last night. The nature of the job meant she'd had to leave it with Dodge at the pizza stall in Piccadilly gardens. Dodge was okay and she trusted him. He'd lived on the streets himself and knew the pitfalls, one of them being not wanting to drag everything you own around with you. He liked Lee and was happy to look after her stuff when asked. Lee shook herself. Time to go, pick up her belongings.

Lee left the alley off Oldham Road where she'd spent the night with the others and headed off. She was hoping to catch sight of the newspaper headlines, see if there was any mention of what she'd done. There wasn't, perhaps it was still too early, but the police were bound to know by now that the Agnew infant was missing.

Thoughts of how to get even with Scott Agnew and the others had filled her head these last weeks. They were responsible for what had happened to her sister Laura, and they'd pay a heavy price. This was only the beginning. Lee had just passed Affleck's when her mobile rang. She jumped, only Joe and Ronzo, the driver from last night, knew her number. She looked at her phone screen. Not Joe. "What d'you want?"

"You're a lucky girl. The boss's got another job for you, and there's twice the money you got last night in it."

"What sort of job?" she asked.

"The type that will interest you."

"So soon on the back of the last one? Won't that make them suspicious?"

"Wrong answer. The boss tells you to do a job, you do it. You're a lucky girl. The Trio is on the boss's hit list as well as yours. You're not the only one with scores to settle. She reckons this city will be a far better place without them." He laughed.

Lee shivered. "Who is it?"

"Someone close to Hutton."

"Close to? Why not Hutton himself? Last night I took the infant, I could have taken Agnew himself. Why play around like this?"

"We don't ask questions, we do as she tells us. D'you want the job, or don't you?"

"Okay, but Hutton has no kids — I checked."

"It's his ageing mother. You up for it?"

A pang of conscience. First a baby and now an old woman. These weren't the people she wanted to terrorise, but what could she do? Lee would never be able to get to these people on her own so she couldn't afford to be choosy. The disappearances would hurt the Trio members, and that's all that mattered. "Okay. When?"

"Meet me in the coffee shop at the bottom of Market Street in ten minutes."

She wasn't far away.

Lee continued walking and within minutes reached the café. Inside, she found herself a window table. Lee sat waiting, biting her fingernails. Joe had warned her to be careful. He reminded her that she'd no idea who Ronzo really worked for, who the person was that wanted rid of the Trio. They were obviously dangerous, and once the job was done Lee herself would be in danger. She had no illusions about that. She knew Joe was right, but she was driven by her need to get even for Laura's murder.

"Hello again." The voice came from the next table. Lee made to turn towards him. "Don't look round," he hissed. "There are cameras everywhere. We don't want anyone who looks at the CCTV to get the impression we're meeting. Better to be on the safe side."

The table was empty when she'd arrived, and he hadn't come in through the main entrance. The back door perhaps?

"Hutton's mother — will she give me any trouble?"

"No, she's an old woman in a care home. I want you to get her out. I'll be waiting in my car on the road outside. You'll get your money once it's done, like I promised, twice as much as last night. When I've gone, pick up the carrier bag I'll leave under the table. Everything you need is inside. Meet me outside the multi-storey on Deansgate in one hour and get changed beforehand."

With that he got up and left, without so much as glancing at her as he passed. He wasn't much taller than her and wore an oversized hoodie pulled low over his face. Lee reached behind her and took hold of the bag. Right enough, inside was a uniform with the logo of a care home on the pocket and an identity badge.

Once he'd gone, Lee sat for a while drinking her coffee. The Agnew infant, Hutton's mother. That just left the Blackmores. Their two kids were adults and living in the USA. No way could Lee get to them. It'd have to be either Grace or Brendan Blackmore himself in that case. But which? Lee decided to think about that another time. For now she had to concentrate on the Hutton woman.

CHAPTER SIX

First day back in the office and Rachel was exhausted. Not what she'd planned. After leaving Jed to sort out his problem, it took her a good hour to get little Len settled. By the time her head hit the pillow, it was hardly worth the effort — a couple more hours and she'd be at work.

"James Agnew," she began, addressing the team at the morning briefing. "Two months old and snatched last night by the babysitter." Saying it out loud like this made her shudder all over again. It would be a nightmare for any parent and having an infant herself, Rachel felt the mother's distress keenly. She wasn't so sure about Agnew himself. Given his reputation, her instincts told her there had to be something he wasn't telling them, and that could be key to finding James.

"The parents were out for dinner, they left at eight. We reckon the sitter left the apartment with the infant about an hour afterwards." She looked at DC Amy Metcalfe and smiled. "Amy — Scott Agnew. Find out what we've got on him. We know he's linked to organised crime in this city but he's so far up the chain of command that he's not fallen foul of the law. On the surface he comes across as a successful businessman. He has money, a posh apartment and the young trophy wife, but knowing what we do, I suspect a lot of his wealth was got by criminal means. Dig deep. It might well be someone linked to that side of his life who is responsible for this."

"Has there been a ransom demand, ma'am?" Amy asked.

"I've appointed Wendy Jackson as the FLO. I spoke to her earlier and she says not." Rachel looked at DC Jonny Farrell. "Last night we met a young lad, a neighbour of the Agnews. He took down the registration of a vehicle that was waiting outside to take the baby away. The sitter didn't get in the car, she ran off. I've got people looking at the CCTV. They might be lucky and pick her up. The sitter also left behind a piece of chewing gum in a bin. Jude and her team have that. Hopefully, we might get a DNA match. The minute that registration number is traced, get on it, Jonny."

Finally she turned to Elwyn. "You and I will visit 'Safe Hands' nursery," she said looking at the card Agnew had given her. "They're in Ancoats." She looked round at them all. "We'll meet here later to discuss our findings."

The team returned to their desks. "Good to have you back, ma'am," Jonny said. "Things haven't been the same without you."

Rachel smiled. "You had Nell and her oppo, Rio. Good detectives, the pair of them."

"No sense of humour though," Jonny said. "Couldn't raise a laugh between them."

"I might be back, Jonny, but I'm in no mood for joking around either, believe me."

"Glad to hear it," a voice said behind her. "Before you get on, we should have a word."

It was Superintendent Mark Kenton. He'd come into the office quietly, a shadow at the door, watching and listening. Rachel felt a shiver slip down her spine. Sometimes she found Kenton a bit creepy.

"I'll be with you in a minute," she said.

* * *

"I've read Sergeant Pryce's preliminary account of last night's kidnap," Kenton said. "The incident is unsettling on a number of levels."

"You don't have to tell me. First and foremost, we have to get the infant back."

Kenton looked dubious. "Agnew," he began. "He's one of the Trio, the crime barons who head up one tight and very efficient operation in this city. They're good at what they do and clever. They've cultivated influential friends too, which is what's kept them out of prison. To date we've been unable to get a thing on any of them. The people who operate below these three do so in fear of their lives. None of them will speak to us because retribution for breaking the rules is brutal. Their workforce don't just go in fear for their own lives but those of their family too." He paused, giving Rachel a smile. "Things were bad enough back in McAteer's days, but believe me, these three are far worse."

Rachel stiffened. He could never resist bringing Jed into it, determined not to let her forget about Jed's background. Ignoring the comment, she asked, "What about the other two in this 'Trio,' as you call it?"

"Ray Hutton and Brendan Blackmore. My advice — along with any enquiries you make into Agnew — check out the pair of them too."

"How long have they been operational?" she asked.

"Several years, but nothing major until about three years ago when they made their move and took over most of the organised criminal activity in the city."

"You think someone has made a stand? Wants them out of the way?"

"I don't know what to think, except that I wouldn't want to be in their shoes when the Trio's people find them. The last individual that crossed them lived but was left so badly injured that he lost a leg and a kidney due to the beating. And an eye and an ear — the result of one of Agnew's people taking a blowtorch to his face."

Rachel winced. "Nice people. I spoke to Agnew last night. Next time, I'll bear in mind what you've just said."

Kenton smiled. "Just mind your back. And a word of advice, keep your association with Jed to yourself. Blackmore and he have history, so I'm told."

CHAPTER SEVEN

Rachel returned to the main office and gave Amy two more names to research — Hutton and Blackmore. "Right, Elwyn, let's make tracks. We'll speak to the nursery in Ancoats and then visit the Agnews again. We can find out from Wendy Jackson what the pair have been up to since she moved in with them."

"What did Kenton want? Not hassling you already, is he?" Elwyn asked as they made their way to the car park.

"He told me about Agnew and his two friends, Hutton and Blackmore. Apparently, things have got a bit hectic out there while I've been away, and they're responsible."

"Kenton must have inside knowledge that he's not shared with us because their names haven't come up in our investigations. We've certainly seen an increase in violent crime, drug-related mostly and highly organised. The people we've brought in haven't been the brightest, so we reckoned there had to be someone at the top pulling the strings."

"I'm thinking the Trio. Have you arrested anyone I might know?" she asked.

"Certainly not a member of that threesome or anyone connected to them. We had a right nutcase in the cells a couple of weeks ago. He was picked up with a small fortune in crack on him. He was offered a deal to tell us what he knew but still wouldn't say a word. He preferred a spell inside. He reckoned that way he'd live and so would his family."

"Kenton reckons the new regime is brutal. The gangs who work for this Trio are too terrified to cross them, like your nutter," Rachel said.

"Hardly surprising about the infant then. Someone making a point. What does Kenton think?"

"He didn't say, just warned me to keep shtum about Jed. He and Blackmore have history, apparently."

"In that case you should heed his advice," Elwyn said. "You can do without the aggro."

'Safe Hands' was a day nursery situated off Redhill Street in Ancoats. It was on the ground floor of a mill conversion and had a view of the Rochdale canal. The owner was a woman called Heather Wright.

Rachel introduced them and asked about the Agnew baby.

Heather smiled. "James. Sweet child, no bother at all. We provide a sitter for his parents occasionally and James's name is down to come to nursery here when he's a little older."

"James was kidnapped last night," Rachel told her. "A sitter called Kate took him from the Agnew apartment. She said she was from here."

Heather Wright shook her head vigorously. "Poor Louise, she must be in bits. But I don't understand, we have no one called Kate working here. Last night's booking was cancelled. We had a call yesterday morning to say that Louise wasn't well and didn't need us anymore."

"Nonetheless, a sitter did turn up," Rachel told her. "A young woman, wearing one of your tabards and with an identity badge."

"Well, it wasn't one of our girls," Heather Wright insisted. "I'm sure of that. They've all been here for some time, all are CRB checked and I trust each and every one of them."

"D'you remember who took the call?"

"Melanie."

"Could we speak to her?" Rachel asked.

Heather Wright gestured to the woman sitting at the reception desk. "The call from Mrs Agnew to cancel, was it her you spoke to?"

Melanie shook her head. "No, the woman I spoke to said she was a neighbour. She said Mrs Agnew had a bad migraine and wouldn't be needing us."

Rachel nodded. "Thanks. Who else would have known about the booking?"

"We use an electronic booking system," Heather Wright told her. "I have access, and so does Melanie." She looked around at the busy room. "To be honest, anyone could have gone into the office, looked at the computer and checked the bookings. I've never had a reason to keep it secret. As I told you, my staff are trustworthy. They have all had the required checks for looking after children and love the job. No one employed here would harm any child, never mind resorting to kidnap." She looked quite angry.

"Nevertheless, I'd like a list of all your sitters," Rachel said. "My team will have to speak to them." She handed the woman a card. "Meanwhile, if you think of anything else, ring me."

* * *

"What d'you think?" Elwyn asked.

"Nice little nursery. Good ratio of staff to children, plenty of equipment, just what I'm looking for in fact," Rachel said.

He shook his head. "That's not what I meant."

"I know what you meant, Elwyn." She grinned. "I think they're straight. Whoever sent that sitter wasn't connected with 'Safe Hands.' It must be someone linked to Agnew's murky dealings. But that nursery is a good one and I wish it was nearer to where I live. I wouldn't hesitate to send Len there, no bother."

"He's already in a nursery, one much closer to where you live."

Rachel pulled a face. "It's okay in an emergency but there's something wrong with the place, the staff don't stay five minutes. One of them told me the manager's difficult to work for and is constantly screaming at the kids. That's no environment for Len."

"You work odd hours and so does Jed. Other than give up work altogether, what choice d'you have?" Elwyn said.

"I was thinking of hiring a nanny." Seeing the look he gave her, she said, "Why not? Jed's got the money, and it would certainly ease my mind."

CHAPTER EIGHT

Scott Agnew wasn't at home. He'd left a weeping Louise being comforted by Wendy Jackson.

"He doesn't give a damn about James," Louise snapped at Rachel. "Business comes first with him. It always will."

Rachel nodded at Wendy. "Go and have a break. I'll speak to you shortly." She deserved it. The job of FLO to the Agnews must be no picnic. For reasons of his own, Scott Agnew was of no help and Louise was understandably too wrapped up in her own distress.

"When we spoke last night, you said you thought James was missing because of something your husband had done," Rachel said to the young woman.

Louise's head shot up. "I was wrong, in shock. What could Scott possibly have done to cause this?"

She was covering for him. Was it out of loyalty or had he threatened her? "Is he pressurising you to backtrack on what you said?"

"Not at all," Louise said at once. "Like me, Scott has no idea why this has happened." She wiped her face. "It's just that his constant fussing over that business of his gets on my nerves, particularly at times like this."

"There's no one he's upset? A business rival or someone else who's threatened you? Could this be punishment for a deal gone wrong, for example?"

Louise Agnew glared at Rachel, her eyes glittering with unshed tears. "No! You've got this totally wrong."

This wasn't getting them anywhere, so why not throw the names into the mix? "Have you ever met Ray Hutton or Brendan Blackmore?" Rachel asked.

Louise's eyes widened. "Why? What have they got to do with James's kidnap?"

"I don't know. I was hoping you might be able to tell me a little about them. Is there currently any ill feeling between those two men and your husband?"

"Of course not. They're business partners, that's all. I've met Blackmore once. As for the other one," she shrugged, "I wouldn't know him if I fell over him."

"The three of them run the property development business, I understand. Are they involved in anything else?" Rachel asked.

"Like what?"

Rachel shrugged. "Anything else your husband is also into."

"Are you talking about other businesses?"

"Yes, the more profitable ones," Rachel said. "Come on, Louise, you must know what sort of man your husband is."

This made Louise prickle. "I don't like your tone. What are you insinuating?"

"If we're to get James back, then you need to tell us everything, even if what you tell me is detrimental to Scott."

"Whatever you're thinking, you're wrong," Louise retorted. "Scott's a good man. He's a property developer not a gangster." She stared at Rachel. "I'm not stupid, you know. That is what you're trying to say, isn't it?"

The woman seemed genuinely upset and angry. Rachel needed to take the heat out of the conversation. "Okay, I'll have a quick word with Wendy and then we'll leave you in peace."

She went into the kitchen where Wendy Jackson was sipping a mug of coffee. "Has either of them said anything?"

Wendy shook her head. "Nothing helpful, but he did get a couple of calls on a mobile he hadn't told us about. I mentioned it, said he should let the team trace the calls, but he ignored me and just put it back in his pocket."

Rachel made a mental note to chase that one up next time she spoke to Agnew. "Has anything been delivered? No note?"

"No, nothing. No ransom demand, no contact from the kidnappers. It makes me wonder why they took the mite in the first place."

Rachel nodded. It didn't look like the reason was money, and that didn't bode well. "Keep your eyes and ears peeled. Anything bothers you, ring me."

* * *

She and Elwyn returned to the station for the team briefing. Both Amy and Jonny had been busy.

"That car registration is fake, ma'am," Jonny told them. "But Andrew gave us the make, model and colour, so that might help."

Rachel was doubtful. "Get an image of the girl?"

"Yes, I've looked at the CCTV from the corridor outside the apartment. She was careful, dressed head to toe in black, the hood of her top pulled down low over her face and with no hair visible. She's wearing gloves so no chance of any prints. But I did see her spit out the gum."

"If she has a record, Jude will get a name. Anything else?"

"There is a camera outside on the street. It got a good shot of the car that picked up the girl, the one that flashed its lights at her. The image was good enough for me to confirm that Andrew was correct about the make and model, but not so clear that I could make out the driver. All I can say is that it was a male. The girl carried the infant in its car seat towards it and fastened the kid into the back seat. She kept her back to the camera and her head down. He drove off towards the city and she legged it down the back streets of Ancoats. I've checked the CCTV in the surrounding area but couldn't pick either of them up again."

Rachel nodded. "Thanks, Jonny. Amy, what have you got on Agnew?"

"He's been brought in a couple of times in the past but nothing these past three years."

"What had he been up to?" Rachel asked.

"On both occasions he was stopped for speeding and a small amount of crack was found on him. He pleaded ignorance, said he hadn't a clue where it had come from. It was a company car and could have been put there by any one of his employees. As for Hutton, he was involved in a jewellery shop robbery in the city centre ten years ago. He wasn't so lucky, he served a short sentence. The shopkeeper was belted around the head but that was found to be down to another of the robbers. Blackmore was charged with tax fraud, but nothing came of it. Fancy footwork by his accountant and legal people, and it was put down as a genuine error. He's the oldest of the Trio and has a heart problem."

"Any hint of what they're up to now?" Rachel asked. "According to Kenton, they're running Manchester. Nothing happens without their say-so, not dealing or anything else. Surely there must be something."

Amy shook her head. "Not that I can find, ma'am."

Rachel sighed. "Okay. Elwyn, we need to look at Agnew's bank accounts, both personal and business. I want to know how much his legitimate business earns. Does it finance his current lifestyle, for example? If a ransom demand is made and he pays it, we need to know. Make that the reason when you ask the magistrate for a warrant."

"Rachel, could I have a word?"

Kenton was creeping about again. He'd entered the office without her noticing him and was listening to the feedback.

"Your office?" Rachel asked, turning round. He nodded. The look on his face said it all. The man wasn't happy.

CHAPTER NINE

The car pulled up at the side of the road and Ronzo turned off the engine. "You've got fifteen minutes," he told Lee. "Go and get the old woman. I'll wait here."

Lee looked at the expanse of garden and the huge property beyond. "How am I supposed to find her? Just look at the size of the place."

"Here's a photo." He held it out to her. "Her name's Edith. At this time of day she'll be in the conservatory having afternoon tea — it's that glass building over there. She'll be in her wheelchair. All the residents wear a name badge, so you shouldn't have much trouble finding which one she is. I don't want any slipups. Get this wrong and the boss won't be happy."

She snatched the photo from his hand. "After this, I'm done. Make sure you tell your boss that. So far, we've wanted the same thing, been out to get the same people, but from now on if I set my sights on anyone else, I'll sort it myself."

"That's not how it works. You're involved with us now and people don't get to just walk away. Anyway, I don't know what you've got to complain about. You're getting what you want and the money's good, a lot better than begging on the streets."

He was wrong. Lee didn't want to kidnap infants and old women. She wanted the three members of the Trio dead. Once she'd finished here, the streets were far preferable to any involvement with this lot. Granted their partnership had been beneficial so far, but it wasn't getting Lee what she really wanted.

Lee got out of the car. She was wearing the uniform and the lanyard with the identity badge dangling from it strung around her neck. Now she looked like all the other carers working here. If she was lucky, no one would take much notice. There must be loads of staff coming and going in a place like this.

She folded her arms and walked towards the gates. A quick backward glance. Ronzo was watching her, and this time wasn't wearing a hood. Lee tried to commit his features to memory — it might be useful. She put him in his early twenties, with a beard and of medium build. If she crossed him, would he know how to handle himself?

Lee shuddered. When this was over, no way did she want to continue her liaison with him and those he worked for. She'd get the old woman and then make her own way back to the city.

As she walked across the lawn, Lee took her mobile from her pocket and rang Joe. "You okay? No one hassling you?"

"I'm fine, hanging out around the gardens with Sponger."

The gardens he spoke of were Piccadilly Gardens in the centre of Manchester. Spending time with Sponger was bad news. He worked for a small-time dealer and would shop his own mother if he thought there was money in it. If Joe were to tell him about the people after her, Sponger could get them both into a lot of trouble. "You should be more careful who you mix with. He's got some dodgy friends. Get on the wrong side of those gangsters and you know what happens."

"Get off my back, Lee. You know nothing about him." He cut her off. Well, she'd tried. Vulnerable as he was, she couldn't babysit Joe for ever. The minute this was done, Lee intended to go into hiding until she'd decided on her next move. After that, she'd disappear. It was only a matter of time before Joe would have to sort things for himself anyway.

A woman gave her a friendly wave, another carer in a uniform. "Matron wants us in the hall later, another of her pep talks." She grimaced.

Lee nodded. She could pull this off. All she had to do was keep her nerve. The weather was mild, and the conservatory doors were open. A group of a dozen elderly women were seated in a semi-circle, some on chairs, some in wheelchairs, each with a blanket over their knees. There was a woman serving cups of tea. She gave Lee a smile and nodded at one of the women.

"Florrie's due her medication. If you fetch it now, she can take it with the tea."

Lee nodded, but her eyes were flicking round the women, frantically searching for Edith.

"Can I have more sugar, love?" One of them asked holding out her cup.

"No, she can't," the woman serving replied sharply. "Strict diet until she sees the doctor next week."

Lee gave her an apologetic smile. "Sorry." She knelt down next to her. "Is Edith here?" she asked.

"Sat at the end, love, in the blue cardigan."

Lee got to her feet and patted the woman's shoulder. "Thanks." She walked towards Edith, who was gazing at the garden outside and humming quietly to herself. A quick glance round — the woman serving the tea had gone. "Fancy a walk, Edith? Let's have a closer look at that flowerbed, shall we?"

Lee pushed the wheelchair out onto the path and towards the main gates. Edith didn't seem to mind, she simply settled back and closed her eyes. Lee planned to get her money then hand Edith over. She would tell Ronzo that she'd make her own way back, and disappear. If he got difficult, refused to pay up, she'd complain, make a scene. Someone from the home would be bound to see and hear. He wouldn't take that risk.

He got out of the car. "Good girl. The old woman is as quiet as a mouse, she looks no trouble at all."

Lee held out her hand. "I want my money. I've done what you wanted, now I'm off."

He laughed. "Don't trust me much, do you?"

Lee watched him take the roll of notes from his pocket. "The boss will want to use you again. Don't imagine for one moment that you can just cut and run. It doesn't work like that."

She looked back at the home. One of the carers was out on the lawn calling Edith's name. Lee snatched the notes from his hand. "She's been missed already, you don't have long. I wouldn't hang around if I was you," she shouted, and took off.

"Have it your way, but don't say I didn't warn you," he shouted after her.

As she ran, Lee stuffed the money into her pocket. She heard Edith screaming and saw the carer turn to look at Ronzo's car. Lee took the first turn and found herself on a large housing estate. Minutes later, she sat crouched down inside a bus shelter. Even if Ronzo came this way he'd not spot her. Lee's plan was to get back to Manchester, collect her rucksack and disappear.

CHAPTER TEN

Kenton gestured to the chair opposite his. "Sit down, Rachel. How's the case going? Got any leads on the infant yet?"

"No more than you just heard at the briefing," she said. "Why, has Agnew been hassling you?"

Kenton ignored the sarcasm. "No, not him but there has been a call to the ACC from the wife of another member of the Trio."

That threw her. Which of the three was in trouble now? "What, about the Agnew case?"

"No. Brendan Blackmore is missing. His wife, Grace, rang the ACC and reported it. Apparently, they're old friends, can you credit it?" he scoffed. "The current ACC is new in the job, one Clare Lansing. Her and the Blackmores were neighbours at one time."

Rachel smiled. "Rather embarrassing for a woman chasing a high-flying police career."

"No more so than you and Jed," he said dryly. "Blackmore hasn't been seen for two days. Not unusual for the man apparently, he often takes off with his fishing mates. But this time none of his usual group have seen him and his wife can't reach him on his mobile."

"Blackmore? What're you thinking?"

Kenton shook his head. "I don't know what to think. Blackmore, Agnew and Hutton are the untouchables, the top layer of Manchester's gangland. No one messes with them."

"Until now," Rachel said. "Someone obviously wants to punish them for something." She felt a flicker of fear slide down her spine. She had a bad feeling. Could that someone be Jed? Rachel had no reason to think that and didn't know where the notion had come from, but it was there, nevertheless. And it scared her.

"Punish, that's an interesting choice of words. Any reason for saying that?" Kenton said.

"No, but the Agnew infant has been taken and there's been no ransom demand, No one's asked for money or anything else. Given who they are, I'd say punishment was definitely something we should look at. What d'you think is going on?"

"I'm keeping an open mind for now," Kenton said. "But someone will have to speak to Grace Blackmore, get the details about her husband, and if he doesn't turn up, we will need to investigate."

"He's an adult. He's free to disappear if he chooses. Perhaps he's gotten tired of the gangland life and wants a fresh start." She smiled.

"Not Blackmore. Villainy is in his blood, hers too," Kenton said. "Before she married Blackmore, she was Grace Hewitt. No doubt you'll have heard of that family."

She nodded. "But not for some time."

"Her grandfather, old man Hewitt, died and things quietened down," he said.

"What about her own father?"

"No idea who he was," Kenton said. "I doubt anyone else does either, outside the immediate family."

"D'you want me to speak to Grace Blackmore?" she asked.

"No, I want you to accompany me. Be there, hear what she has to say but take a back seat. Are you all right with this? You're just back off maternity leave and Grace is pretty hardcore. I could always take DCI Baxter, leave you to read the report later."

Rachel was surprised and a little put out by this. "Absolutely not. This is my case, Mark. I'm the SIO. Besides this could be related to the Agnew case, and I need to hear what the woman has to say."

"This is no reflection on your ability, Rachel," he said. "Neither does it have anything to do with Grace's relationship with the ACC. It's more to do with your relationship with Jed."

That old chestnut. Rachel thought they'd got beyond that now. Jed had a past, she could do nothing about that, but he'd changed, cleaned up his act. "I don't see why that should be a barrier."

"That's short-sighted of you. If it suits Grace Blackmore's purpose to use it against you, she will."

"But we're trying to help the woman," she protested. "She's asked us to find her husband."

Kenton gave her a conciliatory nod. "I understand your feelings but trust me on this. You're not being excluded in any way."

Rachel wasn't so sure, but there wasn't much she could do about it. "Okay. For now I'll go along with what you want. I am living with the very man who ran this city prior to the Trio. Perhaps Grace will talk to me, see me as an ally."

"No chance, and don't even try. Grace Blackmore is a piece of work. She'll know who you are. Take the lead in this and the woman will make it her business to explore the smallest details of your life. And you don't want that. If she can't find anything to use against you, she'll invent something. With Jed a permanent fixture in your life, that won't be hard, and it's a risk I won't have you take. Trust me, Rachel, she's a woman best kept at arm's length."

"I can take care of myself," Rachel said. "She won't be the first gangster's wife I've interviewed." Kenton glanced at the clock on the wall. She saw the look on his face, he was losing patience. "But I'll do as you ask. I'll come along, weigh her up and check out what she tells us."

"Thank you, Rachel. The Blackmores live in a village not too far from you, Mottram St Andrew. We'll leave in half an hour."

* * *

Rachel returned to the main office. The first thing she did was circle Brendan Blackmore's name on the incident board. "The man's missing," she told the team. "His wife has influence it seems, cosy with the ACC, so it'll be Kenton investigating and me as sidekick."

"Interesting development," Elwyn said. "Particularly if you consider a call we've just taken from Stockport nick. Ray Hutton's ageing mother was snatched from a care home earlier today, wheeled out to a waiting car and driven away, all in broad daylight too. Given it's an incident connected to the Trio, the case has been passed to us. Hutton has authorised the home to give us all the help we need and there's a report on the system."

"The Agnew infant, Hutton's mother and now Brendan Blackmore himself has disappeared." She looked at Elwyn. "Got any theories?"

"Yes, but you won't like it," he said, folding his arms. "I think someone is planning a takeover and is making sure the transition is as smooth as possible. Given the nature of the three incidents, I'd say they've got it wrapped up, wouldn't you?"

CHAPTER ELEVEN

Rachel clambered out of the passenger seat of Kenton's car. She had no idea the Blackmores lived so close to her and wondered if Jed knew. She felt nervous, unusual for her, but this woman had a fearsome reputation and Kenton's little pep talk hadn't helped. From what Rachel had read, Grace had been raised in the backstreets of Longsight by a mother barely out of school and a grandfather who only took an interest when he thought she might be useful to his enterprise. Hewitt had her running drugs before she was out of primary school. A difficult upbringing had made her a hard woman who, by foul means rather than fair, had schemed her way to the top. Marrying Brendan Blackmore had helped enormously. As his wife she immediately gained a respect among the criminal fraternity that would have taken years to earn on her own.

"Is the woman expecting us?" she asked Kenton as they walked up the drive towards the huge house.

"Me, yes. You might come as a surprise."

"I've never met her, so there's no reason she should know me."

"She'll know you all right, Rachel. The Trio will have kept a close eye on Jed these last years."

That bothered Rachel. Did they have Jed's name on this? "Are you sure you've no idea what's going on, Mark? You've heard no whispers about a takeover, something I know nothing about for instance?" She was concerned that Jed was under suspicion and Kenton staying quiet about it. He'd once been where the Trio are today. Did Kenton or anyone else think he fancied another go at being top dog?

He laughed. "No one tells me much these days. Anyway, why would I keep something like that secret? I want this mess clearing up as much as you do."

A mess. So that was how he saw it. Kenton rang the doorbell, and a young woman answered.

Kenton smiled at her. "Mrs Blackmore is expecting us."

The woman ushered them inside and gestured towards the conservatory at the far end of the house. "She's in there."

The room had large French doors open to the garden. Grace Blackmore was sipping tea with a newspaper on her knee. As they entered, she looked the pair up and down and then settled her gaze on Kenton. "Have you found him yet?"

She spoke in an even tone. She didn't seem overly worried about her husband, or was this an act put on just for them? Rachel put her in her mid-fifties. She had straight dark hair with a side parting that hung to her chin. Rachel had never met Grace Blackmore or seen any photos but had formed a picture of the woman in her head. She'd imagined someone tall, thin and immaculately dressed, but she wasn't like that at all. The woman sitting with her newspaper was small and slightly overweight. Her clothes were high street bought rather than the designer wear Rachel had expected, but her fingernails were perfectly manicured. Hands not used to housework. There was no smile, and she had hard, dark eyes, the kind that bored right through you.

"No, we haven't had much luck yet, I'm afraid," Kenton said, and smiled at her. "It would help if you would give us a picture of his habits — where he goes, who his friends are, that sort of thing."

"Sit down," Grace ordered and then turned her gaze on Rachel. "You I know, Kenton, but who's this one?"

"I'm DCI King, Mrs Blackmore," Rachel said.

She looked Rachel up and down, her eyes narrow, then surprised her with, "Call me Grace, everyone does," before turning her attention back to Kenton. "I want him found, brought back home, so don't stint on resources. The old bugger is off on one of his fishing marathons, I just know it. Ask Tom Langton, he runs the fishing tackle shop in the village. That one knows more than he's telling."

"Your husband is a grown man, he's allowed to go off if he chooses," Rachel said.

Grace Blackmore tutted. "You think I don't know that? Believe me, young woman, in the past I'd have been glad of the peace but now the old fool has a heart condition, he's on medication which he's left behind and he's already missed several doses. I'm concerned and want him back home as quickly as possible."

Fair enough. "When did you see your husband last?" Rachel asked.

"Two days ago. He left here first thing in the morning. I've no idea what time, I was still in bed." She shook her head. "That's all I can tell you."

"Had the pair of you argued about anything? Was your husband upset perhaps?" Rachel went on.

Grace's head shot up and she glared at Rachel. "You jumped up . . . What are you saying? You think I drove Brendan away? You imagine we spend our time arguing? Well, take it from me, we don't. I can't even recall the last time me and Brendan had a cross word. How dare you come into my home and suggest his disappearance is down to me?"

For a few moments there was real anger in her voice, but suddenly she chuckled. "Make no mistake, I've wanted to throw the old fool out more times than I can remember, but that's just the usual bickering between husband and wife. It doesn't mean anything."

Rachel couldn't decide which Grace was the genuine one, her mood changed so fast. "So the pair of you are sound?" Rachel asked.

"Yes, there's nothing suspicious there, DCI King." She turned her attention back to Kenton. "Find him soon. I want him home and I'm not a patient woman."

"We'll do our best," he assured her. "If you hear from him, you must let us know at once." Kenton fished in his pocket for a card. "Must have left them in the car. Give Grace one of yours, Rachel."

"No," Grace said. "I hear from Brendan, or you get news of him, then I speak to you. I want your work number, mobile and email address."

Overkill, Rachel thought, but Kenton was happy to give her what she wanted. "Okay, I'll go and get one. Give me a minute."

Rachel put her bag over her shoulder, ready to leave as soon as he returned. Being alone with this woman had her on edge. Grace's mood had changed again. For the first time since they'd entered the room, she stood up, moved towards Rachel, took hold of her arm none too gently and pulled her round to face her.

"I know full well what's going on, Rachel." There was menace in her voice. "You tell that man of yours to put this right. The least he can do is return the Agnew infant — and do it quick or there'll be consequences."

Rachel was momentarily stunned. For a few seconds she wasn't sure what was happening or what the woman was on about. At first, she thought Grace was talking about Kenton and then the penny dropped. She meant Jed.

Rachel stared into the angry face, open mouthed. There was no trace of the woman who, minutes before, had spoken lightly about her husband. This Grace Blackmore had venom in her eyes. Suddenly she let go of Rachel's arm and took her by the throat instead.

"Now we understand each other, don't we?" she spat. "You sort this, make it right or you'll suffer the same fate as

Louise Agnew. I'm sure you don't want that. Like her, you too have a baby. Think how it would be if he was taken and you never saw him again." Grace paused, giving Rachel time to take this in. "Make sure you tell Mac and make him listen. You won't get a second chance."

A shocked Rachel prised the fingers from her neck and took a step back. "I have no idea what you're talking about. Do that again and I'll have you charged with assaulting a police officer."

"Don't try that one, lady. It'd be your word against mine and I'm an excellent actress. By the time I've finished it'll be you up on a charge. As for understanding what I'm getting at, you know very well." Grace gave her a sly smile. "If he knows what's good for him, Mac will obey orders. This city doesn't belong to him anymore. Make sure he understands that. You've got kids, consider their safety before crossing me."

'Mac' was the name Jed was known by in the Manchester underworld. Hearing it on this woman's tongue rattled Rachel. She could barely believe what she'd just heard. "You're threatening my family."

"Too bloody true, love, and I don't make idle threats either."

"I'll have you arrested, you can't intimidate me like this and—"

Grace Blackmore shook her head. "Don't you get it? I'll deny every word. Cross me and by the time I'm finished rubbishing your reputation, Kenton will be glad to see the back of you. You'll be branded a troublemaker, which'll put paid to your sparkling career for good."

Kenton was back. He handed the now smiling Grace Blackmore a card. "All the details you asked for are on there. You hear from Brendan, ring me."

Grace glanced at it and tossed it onto the coffee table beside where she'd been sitting. "Good. Now, get out of my house and find my husband. I want daily updates on how you're getting on, understand?"

CHAPTER TWELVE

Rachel didn't feel up to it, but Kenton insisted on stopping in the village and speaking to Tom Langton.

"We're here, Rachel and it's a long way to come back."

But it was a wasted trip. The man hadn't seen Brendan in weeks. From the look of surprise on his face when Rachel said he was missing, she reckoned he was telling the truth.

Detour over they continued the journey back to Manchester in near silence. The visit to the Blackmore home had both upset and angered Rachel. The woman had threatened her family and left her in shock, powerless to do anything about it. They'd been alone, so no witnesses. If challenged, Grace would simply deny everything.

Rachel leaned back and closed her eyes. Kenton had started talking about the case, and about Grace Blackmore, but she couldn't take in the words, they were just so much babble. Her head was full of questions and a growing doubt about Jed. Could the woman be right? Was Jed McAteer making a play for the Trio's position? Was it him who'd arranged the kidnap of the Agnew infant and Hutton's mother? Was he even capable of such acts? Rachel immediately censored the thoughts. She knew him, didn't she? She lived with the man. Whatever he'd once been, these days he was a changed person. They were a family, her and her girls and their baby son. Jed would never risk all that.

Just thinking about Grace sent a shudder down her spine. She was genuinely fearful for her family's safety after what that woman had said to her.

"You okay, Rachel?" Kenton asked. "You look pale."

"Dodgy tummy." A lame excuse, but it'd have to do. "I'd forgotten how crap the canteen food is." No way could she tell him the truth, or anyone else on the team for that matter. First, she needed to discuss this with Jed and quick before she went mad.

Jed McAteer, a one-time gangster much feared in the city, had sworn he'd given up his old ways. He'd tried hard to prove this to Rachel, building a different life, and over the last few years he'd become a successful property developer. If he'd reverted to his old ways, Rachel couldn't understand why. He knew there'd be a heavy price to pay.

"I think I'll get off," she said once they were back at the station. "Tell Elwyn I'll ring him later."

"You okay to drive?"

"Fine. I just need to get home, put my feet up."

She watched him disappear into the building. As far as Kenton was concerned, the visit to the Blackmore house was polite and measured. Grace had given them a few details, she hadn't kicked off, and as far as Rachel could tell the woman was genuinely concerned about her husband. But Kenton didn't know the half of it. The moment she'd got Rachel alone, she'd shown her true colours. For reasons Rachel didn't understand, Grace Blackmore believed Jed was behind the abductions of the Agnew infant, Hutton's mother and now her husband, Brendan. There had to be another explanation.

The drive home seemed endless — the traffic, the thoughts spinning in Rachel's head made for an uncomfortable journey. But finally she turned into the narrow country lane where their house was, and she heaved a sigh of relief.

Her eldest daughter, Megan, lived in a student house near the university she attended in the centre of Manchester, but Mia was home, head in her homework on the kitchen table.

"Jed picked up Len from nursery and he's trying to get him off," Mia said.

Rachel went upstairs to the nursery.

Jed smiled when he saw her. "Shush. He's just gone down. Want some tea?"

"No, I need to talk to you, Jed, and it's important."

"Can't it wait until we've eaten?"

"No. I need to talk now and don't try putting me off. I've had the day from hell and need to ask you a few questions."

He looked concerned. "Okay. What is it?"

Rachel saw the puzzled look on his face. No doubt he was wondering what this was about. She led the way outside into the garden and the summerhouse. There was no way Mia would hear them in here.

"Grace Blackmore threatened our family today." Rachel stood, arms folded, and waited for his reaction. Jed looked bemused and shook his head, but Rachel wasn't having that, he must know who she was. "Grace Blackmore, wife of Brendan, one of the Trio. You know, the band of thugs currently running organised crime in Manchester. Remember her now?"

Jed backed away, his face expressionless. She had no idea what he was thinking.

"She told me you need to put things right or she'll harm our kids."

"I've not seen or spoken to Grace in years," he said. "I can't imagine where this nonsense has come from."

"Well, I can explain that one" She poked her finger into his chest. "She thinks you've kidnapped Scott Agnew's infant son, Hutton's mother, and her husband, Brendan."

Jed shrugged. "The woman is demented. Why would I do any of that? What would I gain by antagonising any of them?"

"I don't know, I'm more concerned about the threat to our kids, and why she thought you were to blame in the first place."

"Well, I'm as confused about that as you are."

From the look on his face, Rachel doubted he was putting on an act. Her manner softened. "What do we do, Jed? How do we fix this?"

He spread his hands. "I've got no idea. I don't move in those circles anymore. I'm straight. Grace knows that but for reasons of her own she's decided to push this one my way."

"You're taking it well," she said. "You look surprised, but you should be livid. Aren't you outraged that she's making threats against our kids?" Rachel had been shaken enough after her meeting with Grace Blackmore but facing Jed, trying to get the truth from him, was worse. She stood, hands on hips, eyes shining with unshed tears. "Please, Jed, speak to me. Have you got roped into something? Tell me what you've done. Whatever it is, we can sort it."

Jed shook his head. "I've done nothing. Grace is spouting a load of rubbish. You can't believe a word that woman says. It'll be some sort of payback for crossing her in the past."

"Like what? How did you cross her?"

"I can't think of anything in particular, but we were always at loggerheads. They were a rival gang, obviously she still bears a grudge."

But Rachel wasn't convinced. "Our kids, Jed, our baby, Len. She looked me in the eye and issued a barefaced threat."

His face was suddenly grey. "Your current case involves the Trio?"

"Yes. It started with the disappearance of Agnew's son. Now things have moved on fast."

Now he looked genuinely worried.

"Can you think of any reason why Grace Blackmore believes you are behind the kidnappings, Jed?"

He shook his head.

"She must think you want back in or why the threats? Her instruction was plain enough — make it right or else."

Rachel left him there and went back into the house. He knew the score now.

CHAPTER THIRTEEN

By the time Lee got back to the city centre it was dark. First stop, the alleyway off Oldham Road where Joe and the others hung out.

"I'm off somewhere else," she told Joe. "This place isn't safe anymore."

"It's fine, Lee. Who's going to notice us here? You're just being paranoid."

But Lee knew different. "A man will come looking. He asks, you haven't seen me in days, got it?"

Joe nodded. "What man?"

"Never mind. Just remember, you don't know where I am."

"This man, does that mean you're in trouble? I can help, you know," he said.

Lee gave him a half-hearted smile. "Leave it, Joe. The less you know the better. And, please, take my advice, get away from here yourself. If they even suspect you know me, you'll come off worst. Better all round if we both just drop out of sight for a while."

"Perhaps you should ask the police for help, Lee," he said.

"Bad idea," she said. "The police won't help me, they're part of the problem. It was you who told me that, remember?"

"That was one detective and a while ago. Things might be different now."

"I doubt that, and I'm not prepared to take the risk. Where there's one bent copper, there are others." She smiled at him. "Better if I just go and lay low for a while."

"Well, okay. I'll hang on with these for a bit longer. My leg's playing up. I'll catch you later."

"Don't forget — anyone comes looking, you've no idea where I am. Tell 'em you've not seen me for days."

"That sounds like you're in big trouble, Lee."

She grinned. "Not yet, but that could change."

The lad shuddered. "You haven't crossed that crew who killed your sister, have you? You might have a temper and the balls to go with it, but they're a fierce bunch. I saw what they did to your Laura, remember."

So had she, the memory was seared onto her brain. Laura had been beaten so badly that the poor girl was practically unrecognisable. She'd been cut too, knifed in the chest and left naked in the open to die.

Lee leaned against the wall, shaking. Sometimes Joe just didn't get it. If only he hadn't brought the subject up. She couldn't cope with the images of her sister's last moments. "What happened to Laura is why I'm doing this, Joe. I live on the streets because it's where I can find out what I need to know."

"I've never asked, generally those of us that live on the streets don't pry into each other's past but what had she done, your sister?" he asked. "Must have been bad for her to end up like that."

She shrugged. "Who knows? She was just fourteen and no threat to anyone. These people are gangsters, drug dealers, they live by their own rules."

Joe looked down at his lower leg. "You don't have to tell me what they're like."

Lee slid down the wall and sat on the ground. She needed a moment. Talking about Laura's murder upset her, left her drained. It brought back so many memories — of how Laura ended up on the streets, of their waster of a father, the death of their mother and the awful row that led to Laura running off that fateful night.

"She should never have left home, Joe. She couldn't cope. Life on the streets was too hard for her. She missed her old life, her friends."

"It wasn't your fault," Joe said.

"Yes, it was. She got hooked on the dope because of me. My friends, my fault. I tried to tell her but it always ended in a right royal row."

Within days of that last stupid row, Lee's sister had lay dying, murdered by a dealer she'd angered trying to steal dope. Like Joe, she'd been beaten, but unlike him, she hadn't been left alive. Laura was made an example of. A warning to any others who might try to cross the new regime.

After Laura's death, Lee kept her head down, listened to the talk on the streets and asked whoever she could trust about who was behind the killing. Joe helped, and it didn't take long for the names Agnew, Hutton and Blackmore to feature prominently in the mix. The big three, as Joe called them, those at the very top of the pyramid. All with solid, blemish-free lives and families. All of them untouchable.

Angry and fired up by Laura's murder, Lee decided to act against them alone. She'd no idea how to go about it, she didn't even know where they lived, but she determined to avenge Laura's murder if it was the last thing she did. Joe offered to help but it was safer for him if he kept out of it. It was about then that he got the phone call.

A man, a stranger, offered to pave the way for Lee to get what she wanted and to make some money in the process. His name was Ronzo. He refused to give any more details or say how he knew about her. But he did say that his boss hated the Trio every bit as much as Lee did.

Lee thought about it for a day or so before deciding to go with it. It was a no brainer really. Ronzo had resources, contacts and the necessary knowledge to achieve what she wanted. Her only worry was whether he was genuine. Given events since, it seemed he was. But the people he worked for were dangerous too and Lee wasn't stupid. Once she'd outlived her usefulness, they'd want her gone.

She got to her feet. "I'm off," she told Joe. "Keep yourself safe." It was raining and all Joe had was his denim jacket. She passed him her old waterproof. She wouldn't need it where she was going. "Here, take this, it'll keep you dry."

Without a backward glance, Lee marched off to collect her stuff from Dodge. From there she'd make her way towards the Oxford Road area. Her idea was to mingle with the student population, she knew one or two of them. She'd met one, a lad called Liam, on a demo a few weeks ago and they'd hit it off. Since then Lee had often seen him about the city. If she was lucky and Liam was feeling generous, he might agree to help her, he might even offer her a bed for the night.

She knew a little about him, that he studied computing at Manchester University. She knew he was clever, talented and that he lived most of his life online. He could have been content with qualifying and getting a good job with a multinational, but Liam had bigger ambitions. His thing was cyber-crime. He'd started by hacking into his fellow students' accounts, pinching their homework. Small-time, nothing too dodgy, but these days he had moved on. Lee had no idea exactly how, but he was making a fortune. She wanted somewhere to hide but she also wanted him to help her find Brendan Blackmore. If anyone could, it was him. Liam worked at the murky end of the web, while with her it was the murky end of Manchester's streets. How well matched they were! A fleeting smile crossed her lips.

CHAPTER FOURTEEN

Back in the house, Rachel busied herself tidying up the baby things left strewn about the place. She needed the distraction to take her mind off the day. Jed came in from the summer-house and followed her around, looking anxious. He seemed genuinely troubled by what she'd just told him.

"Why point the finger at me?" he asked. "That's what I don't understand."

"Well, she must have her reasons. Someone must have said something, tipped her off."

"But there's nothing to tell," he said. "Didn't she say anything else? Give you any clue about where this ridiculous idea came from?"

"No, but she meant every word. She pounced on me the minute Kenton left the room." Rachel stared at him, trying to read the face she knew so well. "Promise me she's either lying or got it wrong, Jed. Please promise me you have nothing to do with this."

He shook his head. "Of course I haven't. I've no idea what Grace is playing at, but I promise you that whatever's happened to the infant, Brendan Blackmore and Hutton's mother is not down to me."

"Then why would she say those things? Why point the finger if it isn't true?" she hissed.

"Who knows?" he said. "I did a bit of business with Brendan years ago, nothing much, but enough for them to know who I am."

"You're saying Grace simply plucked your name out of thin air?" Rachel shook her head. "I don't think so, Jed. That woman is too clever to pull a stunt like that. I believe she knows something, and I intend to get to the bottom of it."

"I'd rather you didn't go near Grace again, Rachel. She's trouble and won't take kindly to having you on her back."

Rachel stopped pretending to tidy up and went up to him, staring into his eyes. "I'm investigating the disappearance of a two-month-old baby, an elderly woman, and now it seems I'm trying to find out what happened to Brendan Blackmore. I have no choice but to speak to the woman. Search that bloody house of hers too if it becomes necessary."

"She won't like that."

"Too bad." Rachel backed off. Mia was standing in the doorway waving her homework at her. She wanted some help. For the sake of peace in their home, she had no choice but to leave Jed for now.

"Be careful, Rachel. Don't let her suck you in." He tapped his head. "Grace has a knack of getting in here. Let's hope Brendan comes home quick and she has nothing more to complain about."

Rachel thought that unlikely. Given what had happened to the Agnew baby and Hutton's mother, there was every chance Brendan had been taken too.

Rachel heard a familiar wail from the nursery. "I'll be through shortly, Mia. Go and play with Len while I finish up in here."

Once Mia was out of earshot, Jed began again. "She threatened the kids? Came right out with it?"

"In as many words, yes. She's one scary woman, Jed."

"Grace is older but obviously hasn't mellowed over the years. But it's possible she's overreacting. All she really wants is her husband back. That pair have been inseparable since their teens. Grace can't cope without him."

"She looked like a very capable woman to me."

"Where Brendan is concerned, Grace is vulnerable. If anything happens to him it'll break her, believe me."

Rachel looked down at the bundle of clothes in her arms. "I wish you lot could be a bit tidier when I'm not here. Mia can help, you know."

"She told me she's got exams."

"Mia will say anything to get out of doing chores. You have to push her, Jed."

"Look, I'm sorry you've had a bad day, and I will speak to Mia, but right now I have to go out."

Rachel was losing patience. "Again? You were out last night. What's going on?"

"Well, I haven't got another woman if that's what you're worried about." He grinned. "Just a bit of business I need to see to."

His words echoed around in her head. Rachel looked at him. Was it possible she'd got it wrong, and that's what this was all about — another woman? But Jed had worked so hard at making their relationship work.

"Like I said, isn't that what managers are for? You need to make your people understand how things are." Rachel walked through to the utility room and put the clothing she'd collected into the washer. "You promised you'd be hands on, Jed. You said we'd share raising Len. According to you, your business practically runs itself — remember telling me that? And every now and again it would be nice to spend a little time together."

"Sorry, Rachel. It's that damn housing development. We keep hitting problems."

She sighed. "Well, don't be late. Has someone cooked?"

"I made lasagne, it's in the fridge."

Jed left, Mia had rocked Len back to sleep and the house was quiet for once. Mia was now poring over her books in the kitchen and didn't need her mum's help anymore. A plate of food, a glass of wine and an early night. If it wasn't for the nagging doubts, life would be pretty good.

Rachel had a quick shower and got changed. By the time she appeared in the kitchen, Mia had packed her books away.

"Megan rang. She'll speak tomoz, she's gone to a party."

"And you? How's the homework going?" Rachel said.

"It's all finished and now I'm off up to my room to Facetime Chloe and chill."

Rachel poured herself a glass of wine and wandered into the sitting room. The feeling that Jed was up to something was still buzzing round her head. There was a pile of paperwork on the coffee table. She sat on the sofa and picked it up. The usual bills, a letter from Mia's school about the open day, and a couple of bank statements. They were for Jed's business accounts and there was a letter with them.

Rachel looked around furtively, despite being alone in the room. She felt guilty, like she was spying on him. But Jed had left the papers lying around, he obviously wasn't shy about her or Mia reading them.

First, she looked at the statements, and what she saw shocked her, made her wish she'd left them well alone. His business account was heavily in the red. The letter made it plain that the bank wasn't prepared to let the situation continue for much longer.

So, bottom line, Jed had money problems and he'd not said a word to her.

CHAPTER FIFTEEN

Day Three: Tuesday

It was not yet eight, but Clayton Health Centre was already busy. A constant stream of people filed in and out, and there were at least two dozen people waiting to see a doctor or a nurse. Mary Lawton, the practice manager, didn't notice the infant until he started to cry.

"He's been there in that car seat for ages. Not surprised he's howling his head off," a waiting patient told her. "The poor little mite'll be hungry and there's no sign of his mother."

"Did you see her?" Mary asked.

"No, I presumed she'd gone to the ladies, but now it looks as if she's dumped the kid and scarpered."

Mary called to one of the nurses. "Gaby, would you take him to your room and look after him while I see if his mother is with one of the doctors?"

Mary went from room to room asking patients and staff if they knew anything about the baby, but no one did.

"He's called James Agnew," Gaby told Mary when she returned. "There was a note tucked underneath him. Apparently, he's been missing."

"Missing?" Mary said with surprise. "I've not seen any-thing in the papers, and anyway, why leave him here?"

"Someone took him and has since thought better of it," Gaby suggested. "Thought this was the best place to leave him. I guess they knew he'd get looked after in a health centre."

Mary nodded. Gaby's reasoning was sound. "I'll ring the police. If the little lad is missing like the note says, his parents will be frantic."

* * *

When Rachel got up the following morning, Jed still wasn't there. She checked her mobile — no missed calls and no texts either. What the hell was going on? The other woman idea was getting less far-fetched by the minute. She tried ring-ing him, but his mobile went straight to messaging. Other woman aside, there had to be something wrong. This wasn't how Jed usually behaved and, coupled with the grim reading his bank statements made, Rachel was concerned.

Mia was dressed for school and about to leave. "I'm hav-ing tea at Chloe's," she announced. "Don't forget to book your slot online for the open evening. That is if you want to speak to my teachers."

"I most certainly do, young lady. These are important years, exams and all that. Got to keep you on track." Mia didn't ask about Jed, so Rachel didn't say anything. Once Mia had left, Rachel got Len up and fed and dressed him. Jed was still a no show, so it'd have to be another day at the nursery. Sending their son full-time hadn't been part of the plan, but since her return to work, and with Jed's frequent absences, she hadn't had much choice.

Within the hour, Rachel was heading down the A6 on her way to work. She was negotiating the Apollo roundabout when she got the call from Elwyn.

"James Agnew's turned up," he said.

Rachel could barely believe it. "Is he all right?"

"Yes, he's fine."

That was a huge relief. "You sure? It's definitely him?"

"There was a note left with him, tucked into the cushion of the car seat. He's at the health centre in Clayton, left in the waiting room sometime this morning. No one can recall who by. I'm on my way now."

"Is he okay?" she asked again, unable to quite believe this.

"According to the nurse looking after him he was hungry but in perfect health."

"Have the parents been told?" she asked.

"Yes, they'll meet us there."

"That promises to be fun. I can hear Scott Agnew issuing his orders now. A health centre, you said, so there'll be CCTV?"

"The practice manager is sorting it for us," Elwyn said

"Okay, I'll meet you there in about fifteen minutes."

Rachel was relieved that the infant had turned up safe and sound but puzzled as to why the kidnapper had had a change of heart. If there was no ransom demand, why bother to take him in the first place? Taking on the likes of Scott Agnew was a dangerous game.

As Rachel pulled into the car park at the health centre, her mobile rang. It was Jed. Without giving him time to speak, Rachel laid into him. "Where the hell have you been all night? No call, no message, nothing. I was beginning to think something had happened to you."

"Sorry. It's the job, I told you. I had to call people in, get them to work all night in order to meet today's deadline. It needed me there to ensure it all got done properly."

"Is this how it's going to be from now on, Jed? You go missing and I cope. I thought I'd done with managing on my own."

"You were never really on your own, Rachel. You had Alan, remember. Anyway, I've sorted the problem and it won't happen again. The job is almost completed and then I'm all yours."

Easy enough to say, but would Jed keep his word? "Len's at the nursery. You'll have to pick him up. Busy or not, Jed, it's your turn and don't leave him there all day."

She didn't mean to give Jed a hard time but what had started as a niggle at the back of Rachel's mind was growing with every passing hour. He'd never had to stay out due to work before. Now the infant had turned up, Grace Blackmore's words resonated. She'd insisted that Jed put things back the way they were. She'd added weight to her demands by threatening his family. Rachel had told Jed last night, and suddenly the Agnew infant was back. Coincidence? If Hutton's mother also turned up, then perhaps it wasn't.

She sat in her car for a few moments, getting her head together. She had no solid proof that things were not as Jed had told her, but for the sake of her own sanity, she decided to ask him a few searching questions later. Rachel was concerned that his apparent money problems might have forced Jed back to his old ways. If it wasn't that, there was still the other woman to worry about.

CHAPTER SIXTEEN

"The parents have arrived," Elwyn told Rachel as soon as she entered the reception area. "She's just happy to get her son back, but he's out for blood."

Just what she needed on top of the turmoil in her head. Putting on a smile, Rachel approached the couple. "Mr Agnew. James has been returned and none the worse for his experience."

"No thanks to you lot." He glared at her. "Whoever took him left him here. That wasn't down to your investigations."

"We don't know that," Rachel said. "We have spoken to people, perhaps we rattled a few cages. It's possible that whoever took your son thought it wiser to return him."

Agnew chose not to answer. "He's been checked over by one of the doctors here and pronounced fit and healthy, so we're leaving. But I have no intention of letting this drop. I want who did this to us finding and punished."

"Rest assured we're working hard to that end. Since we last spoke, have you had any thoughts on who might be responsible? Someone you know or have business dealings with for example?" Rachel asked.

"No. That's your job."

"Are you aware that Ray Hutton's mother was snatched from her care home?"

"I did hear something," he admitted.

"You and Mr Hutton are business partners. We have to consider that a rival was behind this. Perhaps someone you upset recently."

"I'm not given to upsetting people so badly that they'd steal my son, Inspector. Besides, no one we have dealings with would be so stupid."

"Are you also aware that Brendan Blackmore is missing? That's the three senior partners in the firm you run affected. That has to mean something, surely."

"Whatever it means, I can't help you. You need to look elsewhere," he said. "None of this has anything to do with our business."

As far as she was concerned, this had everything to do with his so-called 'business.' A takeover, some smart Alec flexing muscle. She wasn't sure which, but Rachel was determined to find out, if only to rule out any connection to Jed.

"You'll have to leave James's clothing and seat with us," she told the parents. "We'll pass them on to Forensics, see if they find prints or DNA that will help find who took him."

"Is that absolutely necessary?" Agnew said. "What will we dress him in?"

Rachel smiled. "I'm sure the practice manager will help you with that one."

"Now that James is coming home, you can have that Jackson woman back. Her presence in the house is unsettling," he said.

"I'll sort it," Rachel said.

The infant's clothing was bagged up and with him dressed in an assortment of odds and ends found by the practice staff, the two detectives watched the Agnews leave, James safe and happy in his mother's arms.

"I feel sorry for that woman. She's young, and what's the betting she knows very little about what she's married into."

Elwyn held up a memory stick. "She'll find out one day, Rachel. I've got the CCTV. Jonny and Amy are arranging interviews with the staff here and all the patients who've been in the waiting room this morning."

Rachel nodded. "Good work."

"Back to the office, strong coffee and give the CCTV a look at?" he said.

Rachel nodded. The coffee would be more than welcome. Yet again, she'd hardly had a wink of sleep, too worried about Jed and what he was up to.

"You okay?" Elwyn asked as they made for the cars. "We've had no time to chat since you've been back, but you do seem a bit preoccupied. Coping all right, are you?"

"Preoccupied is one way of describing it." She sighed. "Truth is, Elwyn, I'm going out of my mind with worry about any number of things."

"Can I help?"

A kind offer and Rachel would like nothing better than to confide in him, but she daren't. "Some of it is personal, so it wouldn't be fair to burden you. What's bothering me might have repercussions. Better if you don't know."

If Jed was up to his old tricks, she was hoping to stop him before it got out of hand. She wanted to do a little more investigating before she faced up the consequences. She needed to prove that Jed had resumed his criminal ways and was responsible for what had happened. If he had, the repercussions could be catastrophic both for him and her career. Finding that there was another woman on the scene would almost be a relief.

"Let's hope the Hutton woman turns up too."

Rachel nodded. "Returning her won't be as easy. From what I read in the report, she's in that home because of a physical impairment and is perfectly well mentally. That means Edith Hutton would be able to tell us what happened, who took her and where she's been. I can't see the kidnapper wanting that."

CHAPTER SEVENTEEN

Grace Blackmore led her two guests into the sitting room and gestured to the drinks cabinet. "Help yourself to drinks and take a seat. You both know why you're here."

"I got a call this afternoon," Hutton said. "Unregistered mobile, so no use even trying to trace it. Their demands were made clear. Instructions will follow, so the message read."

"I was sent a list of demands and a photo." Grace picked up her mobile from the coffee table and passed it to the two men. The image showed her husband tied to a chair and with tape over his mouth. "He looks tired and bruised about the face. The animals have hurt him."

"But it does mean they're both still alive," Hutton said. "You sure that's Brendan?" he asked handing the phone back. "The quality isn't good, and that tape doesn't make it easy."

"I do know my own husband," she snapped.

"The caller said my mum is fine, but I hope she isn't being held like that. It would be inhuman at her age. She won't cope or understand. She's got all her faculties, but she's old and needs the usual people and her own things around her," Hutton said.

Grace wasn't concerned about Hutton's mother — she had enough worries of her own. "Brendan doesn't have his medication with him. With his heart problem that could be fatal. You run the streets, Ray, what's being said? There must be whispers."

"There's nothing, Grace. Everything is as normal. I've had my people make discreet enquiries, but they drew blanks."

"So what next? Do we just roll over? Give these bastards what they want?" She waited for a response but neither man said anything. "We do that and we're finished. Have you pair forgotten who we are? What we stand for? Our name and reputation used to mean something in this city. Now it seems anyone who fancies their chances can take what they want from us."

"The demands we've been sent make it clear that we refuse to meet them and both Brendan and Edith die," Hutton reminded them.

Grace was losing patience. She expected more from these men, though she was well aware that despite the way the operation was organised, it was Brendan who usually gave the orders.

"I think we give it a bit longer before doing anything. I got my son back this morning. He's home and safe, and that's how I want it to stay," Agnew said. "I reckon the kidnapper got scared, realised who he's dealing with. I'm sure the same will happen with Brendan and Edith. The kidnapper will come to his senses, and they'll be released."

Grace shook her head. "You're an idiot if you believe that. They're adults. Whoever took them can't just let them go, they'll talk, tell us what happened to them." Grace Blackmore sipped on her brandy. "Your son was an exception, Scott. That you've got him back is down to me threatening that detective who's shacked up with Mac. I made it plain what would happen to her kids if he wasn't returned." She dabbed at her eyes with a hankie. "If anything happens to Brendan, if we let him down, I won't cope. We've been together most of our lives and I need him back where he belongs."

Grace knew they'd never seen her like this. She didn't let her feelings show. Well, not her softer ones.

"We mustn't jump to conclusions, Grace." Hutton leaned over and took her hand. "You've spoken to the police about him, they'll be looking for them too."

"I doubt it. I made out that he'd most likely gone fishing. And when did we rely on the police to sort our problems? You've gone soft, the pair of you. I only spoke to them to ensure that that woman of Mac's knew exactly where she stood. Proof, if we needed it, that it is Mac who's doing this to us. He needs teaching a lesson, and that's where we start. We run this city, we're the Trio."

"That's a dangerous game you're suggesting, Grace," Hutton warned. "Get on the wrong side of McAteer and it will be all-out war."

"If that's what it takes because I refuse to fumble around in the dark, be blackmailed and terrified for the safety of our loved ones?" Grace took a moment. She was weeping again. It wasn't like her, and she could see from the look on their faces that neither man knew what to say. "We've become complacent. We've taken our eye off the game and Mac has seized his chance."

Finally she wiped her eyes and sat up straight. "Have you heard the name Nidge Fortune?" Both men shook their heads. "He's a lawyer, been around for about three months and he's working for Mac. He's already approached a couple of our people and warned them off. Told them that certain streets are now off limits to us." She tutted. "The man has some front. Blatantly doing Mac's dirty work."

"McAteer?" Hutton exclaimed. "Are you sure? I thought he'd gone straight, got himself a family."

Grace nodded. "Yes, that's with the detective I mentioned. But make no mistake, Jed McAteer wants back in, wants his old position and territory back. He knows we're onto him. I've met the detective and marked her card. She came here with Kenton after I reported Brendan missing. I spoke to her alone and laid it on the line, told her what would happen if our people weren't returned. She and Mac have recently had a child. I asked her how she'd feel if her infant disappeared." She smiled. "And look what happens. Within hours you get your son back, Scott."

"So, what do we do about him?" Agnew asked.

"We need to know what's happened to Edith and Brendan before we do anything," Hutton replied. "We tackle Mac now and we could lose them for good."

"Not if we snatch one of his nearest and dearest first. He's made demands and we can't just ignore them," Grace said.

"We do that and it's tantamount to signing Edith and Brendan's death warrant."

"I don't know this Fortune person, but I'll make a few calls. Meanwhile do nothing rash. Mac's a dangerous man and obviously willing to take risks to get back what he used to have."

"I said at the time Mac going straight wouldn't last. The man isn't cut out for honest graft."

"He's in debt," Hutton said. "His latest venture is a money pit. Unless he does something, it'll bankrupt him. The last thing we want is that man leeching on our business, attempting to take over the streets we run. If he's planning a takeover, he'll need a fortune to set things up. Ask yourselves, where's that sort of money coming from?"

"Read the demands he sent. He's not interested in our money," Grace said. "Everything's changed since his day. The people he knew and dealt with are long gone. Mac wants information, the names of our contacts, the nitty gritty of how we operate. He wants everything he needs to take over from us. If we don't agree, then what's the betting we don't see Brendan or Edith again?"

"Does that detective he lives with have any influence?" Hutton asked. "As I said, returning an infant is one thing but my mother and Brendan are a different matter."

"My feelings exactly," Grace said.

"I'm grateful for your intervention, Grace, but we can't just give him what he wants. Disclose the names of our operatives, our procedures, we'll be left with nothing," Agnew said.

"Not quite nothing. At least that way there's a chance we'll get the hostages back," Grace said. "Right now that's my main priority, and Ray's too. Brendan means more to me than running Manchester's streets."

"So what do we do now?" Hutton asked.

"We could beat whoever is doing this at their own game."

"You're talking kidnapping Mac's kids again," Agnew said. "That will just complicate things. If this is down to Mac, then he has an agenda and he'll stop at nothing, kids in danger or not."

Grace still wasn't so sure, in her book it was till worth a try but for the time being she'd go along with the consensus. "Whoever sent the messages wants to deal with me alone," Grace said. "But I have no idea what to tell him. I don't know enough about the operation."

"All these years working together and none of us knows about the other two's part of the operation — their procedures, contacts, nothing," Agnew pointed out. "It's how we all wanted it back in the beginning. It's meant that we can rely on each other, operate in complete trust."

"Given what's happened, surely you see that it's one huge vulnerability," Grace said. "With Brendan absent, a gap has suddenly opened up."

"What d'you mean?" asked Agnew.

"In the way we run things. The strict demarcation of roles and intelligence does us no favours." Grace watched the two men. The look on their faces said they weren't impressed by her criticism. "Brendan is responsible for liaising with our people overseas, negotiating deals, buying the drugs we bring into the country to sell on the streets. Do you know who these people are, or what countries they come from?"

"No, but that's how it's always worked," Hutton said. "It was set up that way because of trust issues. Back in the beginning we didn't know one another. We were scared witless about being double crossed."

"Well, we all know each other now, don't we?" Grace smiled. "So that aspect is redundant. What happens if Brendan doesn't return? Who will negotiate with our foreign partners then? Eh? We three here don't even have one name between us." She turned to Agnew. "Scott, you take care of transport from the docks all along the coast. You have people working there on our payroll. Neither I nor Ray have any idea who they are. You, Ray, have control of the streets, distribute the goods and run a small army of dealers. Again, Scott and I know none of these people and wouldn't know how to contact them."

"How does that make us vulnerable?" Agnew asked. "No one has overall control, each has their discrete slice of the business and that has always been a positive."

"And it's worked well. But don't you see the gaping holes in a set-up like that? We can't continue without Brendan. For all we know, the information has been beaten out of him. And without it, we don't have a business."

"I'll have to think about it," Hutton muttered.

"While you're at it, think of Edith and what she's going through," Grace retorted. "If you'd prefer, we could go round to Mac's house and beat her whereabouts out of him. Perhaps spirit away one of his family, that would show him."

"He returned my son," Agnew said. "You must have this wrong, Grace."

"Yes, Grace, he's right," Hutton added. "I don't want to antagonise Mac until we know for sure he's behind the kidnaps."

"With respect, Ray, the longer we delay the harder it'll be to get back what's ours. Before we know it, Mac'll be the one with dope to sell, not us."

The two men fell silent while they considered her words.

"You're right," Agnew said finally. "It's a takeover and the bastard has hit us where we're weakest." He looked at Grace. "What now?"

"We wait, let the blackmailer, be that Mac or whoever, make the next move. In the meantime, you both consider your part in our operation. When I'm asked, I'll need names, procedures, the lot. The time has come to let each other in."

"I'm not sure," Hutton said. "And anyway, without Brendan's information what we know is useless."

"Just do as I ask, both of you. Sooner or later I'll have to give whoever's doing this something. I'll be careful, offer a couple of crumbs. He'll be sure to check them out, so what he gets has to be genuine."

"The police might find them both before then," Hutton said.

"I doubt it. They've no idea where to look and they don't suspect Mac," Grace said.

"We could put that right, give them a couple of pointers. Do we still have our detective onside?" Hutton asked.

"Yes," Grace said. "We can get the help we need, for a price. No one has anything to gain from Mac rising to the top, including the police. Hopefully, we get Edith and Brendan back and then we'll deal with him. Our detective on the inside will make sure he never troubles us again and put the entire incident to bed. There will be no comeback."

CHAPTER EIGHTEEN

It was late afternoon when Rachel and Elwyn returned to the station. Rachel disappeared into her office to ring home. Mia answered.

"Is Jed in?"

"No, he hasn't been back all day."

What was he playing at? What was so important it took all night and most of the day to sort? "I might be late, are you all right to get some food for yourself?"

"No worries, I'll grab a bite then me and Chloe are off out. What're you doing about Len?"

What indeed? Collecting him from nursery was supposed to be Jed's job. "Don't you worry, I'll sort it." The call finished, Rachel rang Jed's mobile. It went to voicemail. Where was he? She was annoyed with him for the disappearing act, but concerned too. This wasn't like him. She had no choice. Rachel was about to drop everything and leave for home when her mobile rang.

"Where the hell have you been?" she blasted Jed, though her anger was mitigated by relief that he was okay. No one had the ability to wind her up like him.

"I've been waiting for the bloke from the planning department. I tell you, these bloody houses are turning out to be more trouble than they're worth."

Rachel was way past listening to excuses. "Are you free now?"

"Yes, love."

"Good, because I'm running late. You'll have to pick Len up from nursery. When I get home, we need a serious talk. You being a hands-on dad just isn't working, is it, Jed? I can't trust you to do your bit."

"That's not fair, Rachel. I've had a lot on. You're not the only one with demands on their time, you know."

He was right. They both needed to apply a lot more give and take. "Okay, we'll discuss it later. Plenty of people have kids and manage to work, we're no different." Rachel finished the call and went out into the main office to get some coffee. A serious talk with Jed later, after which she'd decide whether to send Len to nursery full-time or hire a nanny. Not what she wanted, but given Jed's money problems the choices were limited. Could they even afford it? That was another subject that needed talking about. Jed had never been cash-strapped before, not since he'd been back in her life anyway. He was a wealthy man, so what had happened to change that?

Rachel walked across to the coffee corner, casting a wary eye on the team. Jonny Farrell was studying his computer screen with DCI Baxter watching over his shoulder. Amy was at her desk giggling like a teenager on her mobile. Rachel shot her a look and got a big grin for her trouble.

"Sorry, Mark, got to go," she said loud enough that everyone could hear.

Baxter shot Rachel a knowing grin and made his exit.

"We all make personal calls, Amy, but organising your social life isn't on when we're so busy," Rachel snapped. "Have you sorted those bank statements yet? Do know if the infant was returned with no strings, or did the Agnews pay a hefty ransom we don't know about?"

"His accounts here look fine, ma'am. But I've done a little extra digging and he does have two offshore accounts I can't get access to."

"What sort of digging? Strictly legal I hope."

"I have a contact in Agnew's bank. He gave me the information, ma'am."

Not information they could use then but it was useful to know. "Has anyone looked at the CCTV from the health centre yet?" Rachel asked.

"I'm doing it now, ma'am," Jonny said.

"Sorry about the call, ma'am," Amy said. "It's just that Mark wanted to know where I'd like to eat later."

"Mark Kenton?"

Amy nodded.

"It's a dangerous game you're playing, Amy. He's a senior officer in this nick, and if your relationship comes to the attention of the wrong pair of eyes, it'll be you who suffers. Mark will cover his back, believe me. DCI Baxter heard every word of that conversation, who's to say he won't go blabbing to anyone who'll listen."

"Mark will bring him to heel. He likes me, ma'am, and I him. Things could get serious."

"Don't get sucked in," Rachel said. "Think of your career, your future."

"Mark has promised that I'll do just fine. He wants me to go for sergeant soon."

What was the use? Amy saw only what she wanted to see. Rachel made herself a mug of coffee and returned to her office. She had plenty to think about without Amy's love life.

"It won't last, Kenton'll get bored. Men like him usually do," Elwyn said, sticking his head round the door.

"She's a fool but if she won't accept advice, there's nothing we can do about it," Rachel said.

"I've got something, ma'am," Jonny said, joining them.

"Right, let's take a look."

The three of them walked across to Jonny's desk and focused their attention on his computer screen.

He pointed to a figure. "See? The person coming into the waiting room is carrying the car seat with the kid in it. The little lad looks to be asleep. The seat is put down where it was later found and the figure leaves." Jonny stopped the video with the individual in the centre of the frame.

"Male," Rachel said. "Tall and well built."

"Not the girl who took him then," Elwyn said. "Means we've got more than one person involved in this."

"He's covered up from head to toe, just like the girl. There's barely anything of him showing. Balaclava, scarf around his mouth, glasses, gloves, the lot," Jonny said.

"Not much chance of finding him from the CCTV in that case. Did the seat go to Forensics?" Rachel said.

"With Jude as we speak," Elwyn replied.

"Did we get any other CCTV from the night the infant was taken?" Rachel asked.

"Nothing helpful," Jonny said.

"What about the care home?" she said.

"We got footage that shows the back view of a woman wheeling Edith Hutton across the grass. Apart from the fact that she had short blonde hair, nothing very helpful," Jonny said.

"Okay, I'll have a word with Jude, see where she's up to." Rachel picked up the phone and called her. "I'm praying you've got something. We're clutching at straws here."

"We're still analysing the car seat. There's not a lot to help, but the infant was sick. There's vomit on the seat and on his clothes. Find a suspect or the vehicle and it's possible some might have transferred. As for prints and DNA other than the child's, I suspect that whoever handled him and his belongings wore gloves. But we have found something on the chewing gum."

"Brilliant. A DNA match to someone we know?"

"I'm afraid not," Jude said.

Rachel was immediately disappointed. "What have you got then?"

"The girl who chewed that gum was a familial match to the teenage girl we had in the morgue a couple of weeks back. If you recall, I mentioned her to you. The rough sleeper who'd been beaten and stabbed to death."

"Was she found on our patch?" Rachel asked.

"Just outside. North Manchester got the case in the end," Jude said.

"How close a familial match?" Rachel asked.

"Sisters," Jude said. "Not what the young woman who came to identify the body told me. A friend was what she said. She did say the dead girl's name was Laura Lomax. All she'd tell me about herself was that her name was Leona but that she was known as Lee."

"Sisters. It's a start," Rachel said.

"And you've got her name — Leona or Lee Lomax," Jude added. "She didn't hang around long enough for us to get much else out of her. Later when I filled out the forms, I would have got more details but I never got the chance. I know the detective from North Manchester wanted a word, but she sneaked off before he had the chance. She didn't give an address either. But from how she was dressed and the fact she had a sleeping bag under her arm, I reckon she was homeless too."

"Thanks, Jude."

Rachel sat and thought about this for a moment. If this Lee was the dead girl's sister and as she'd told Jude she blamed the Agnews for her death, it was a motive for kidnapping the infant. The need to get back at Agnew must have been acute. But that didn't explain the kidnap of Edith Hutton, or Blackmore's disappearance. Organising that would take more resources than a young woman living rough on the streets could muster.

Rachel went back into the main office to update the team. She was about to start the briefing when Kenton called to her from the doorway.

"Could I have a word?" he asked.

CHAPTER NINETEEN

After a few drinks Liam took pity on Lee and agreed to let her stay in his flat that night, though calling the one room with shared bathroom and kitchen a flat was pushing it a bit. There was hardly room for him, never mind a guest.

"There's ten of us share the house," he told Lee. "Most of the others are sound, students like me, but a couple are a waste of space, Dougie next door being one of them, so give him a swerve if he starts asking questions."

"You got any food?"

"No, but you can go to the student union and get a cheap meal," he told her.

"I'm not a student," she said. "They won't let me in."

Liam handed her a badge. "I've printed one out for you, it's even got your photo on it." He smiled at her. "It's a nifty little sideline I've got going. They don't check too closely. It'll get you into the union and the library as well. Which means that if there's any problems, people in here start prying, you'll have somewhere to go that's warm and dry."

"Thanks, but can I sleep here a bit longer?" she asked. "That sofa isn't as lumpy as it looks."

Liam nodded. "Just keep away from the others. Don't invite questions."

Lee was grateful. Liam had provided a safe bolthole until she decided what to do next. Ronzo and those he worked for wouldn't find her here. "You out today?"

He nodded at his laptop. "No, I'm going to do some business on that instead."

"Online? Something dodgy?"

He grinned back. "Very dodgy, but lucrative. My advice, don't ask too many questions."

Lee sat on the not-too-lumpy sofa and rang Joe. She needed to know that he was all right, not got himself into any bother. But he didn't pick up. Not like him, and that set the alarm bells off. "I'm worried that a friend of mine might be in trouble," she told Liam. "He might have been arrested, or the people after me might have caught up with him."

"These people have names?" he asked.

"The bloke who was helping me get even is called Ronzo, but the ones we're fighting are Blackmore, Agnew and Hutton."

Liam gave a low-pitched whistle. "You really do know how to pick 'em. The Trio, Manchester's top gangsters. How in hell's name did you get yourself mixed up with them?"

"They killed my sister," she said bluntly. "It's only fair they pay. The law won't do anything, there's no proof and anyway they've got cast iron alibis. But they are responsible. The men who beat my sister to death and finished the job with a knife were under orders from them. These men who issue the orders are at the top of one huge rotten tree and think themselves untouchable. It's about time they got what's coming, realised no one stays safe forever."

Liam looked doubtful. "You've got a job on there, Lee. My advice, for what it's worth, forget it, walk away, don't mess with those people."

Lee was about to reply when her mobile rang. It was Joe. She replied at once. "Hello, Joe. You all right?"

"Yeah, I'm with the others in the alley."

"You should go somewhere else, lay low like I said."

"Get off my back, Lee. I can get by just fine."

If Joe wouldn't take her advice there wasn't much she could do. "Bye Joe, and remember what I said." She finished the call and put her mobile in her rucksack. He might say he was fine but that was just bravado. In reality, he was terrified of being set on again by those thugs.

"You okay, Lee? You look worried," Liam said.

"I am. That was a friend of mine who can't, or won't, look after himself. Ronzo, the man I've been working with against the Trio will be looking for him. If he finds him, then Joe is in big trouble."

"This Joe, can he handle himself?" Liam asked.

"No, he's got a gammy leg and other injuries — a run in with the Trio's men a while ago. He's no match for any of them now."

"This Ronzo, does he have a proper name?"

"I never knew it." She gave Liam a weary smile. "Not much help, I know."

"I'll do a little digging online, see if anything's being said in the chat rooms."

She looked at the clock on the wall. "The nights are long when you live on the streets. I just hope Joe survives."

CHAPTER TWENTY

"I've had Grace Blackmore on the phone again, asking how the search for her husband is going," Kenton said.

Rachel was sitting with Kenton in his office. "She's worried about her husband. That's natural enough."

"Grace is no ordinary housewife, Rachel. And I don't believe Brendan would just go missing on a whim. First Agnew's kid, then Hutton's mother. I have a bad feeling about Brendan Blackmore."

"Based on what?" Rachel said. "We have no evidence to suggest that anything untoward has happened to him. We have no motive for the kidnaps either. No one has made any demands yet, and the Agnew child has been returned."

"No demands that we know of, Rachel," he pointed out. "They're a close bunch that lot. But Grace is right, we must make some progress soon. Hutton's mother is old, she needs care and attention, and if she doesn't get it, she won't survive. And Brendan has a heart problem, he needs his meds or things could be bad for him too. Speak to Hutton, see if he can help, if he's heard anything. Stockport station said there had been no ransom demand, but we need to be sure."

"I'll get on it, but if he knows nothing and the kidnappers don't return her like they did with the infant, then we've got precious little to go on."

"Anything happens to Hutton's mother or Brendan Blackmore and this city will erupt. There'll be a drugs war and the streets will be a battleground for the different gangs waiting in the wings for just such an event. Whoever comes out on top might well be a lot worse than the Trio."

Rachel looked at Kenton. What did he know? What wasn't he saying? "You've heard something. That look on your face. I've worked with you long enough to recognise it."

He hesitated. "I did hear a whisper."

"Come on then, tell me."

"You won't like it, Rachel."

Now she was annoyed. "Like it or not, that's not the point. Spit it out, Mark."

"My informant reckons it's an inside job. I've been sitting here trying to work out which of them has the most to gain. In the end I decided on Grace."

"You think Grace wants to run the entire show?"

He smiled. "I don't know why you look so shocked. Grace is a better choice than my first contender."

"Who was that?"

"Jed."

"That's a ridiculous idea and you know it. I don't understand how you can sit there and accuse him."

"He's broke."

The words hung in the air as Rachel stared at him. How did Kenton know that?

"A situation he's not used to or happy with. Jed needs to get his hands on a shed load of money to finish his current projects. He doesn't find it, his business goes bust, Rachel."

"Jed has been in property development long enough to know the pitfalls and avoid them. I don't believe he'd back a loser, Mark."

"The houses he's trying to build on that brownfield site in Clayton are giving him one huge problem. First, he discovered the land was contaminated. That cost a bundle to sort. The next problem was finding out that there's an old mine workings under the site. There's every possibility that the entire tract of land those houses are built on will sink into oblivion. With that hanging over them, buyers are non-existent. No bank will give a mortgage on such a prospect."

Jed was a sound businessman, he'd made mistakes early on and learned from them. He wouldn't take on something as risky as Kenton had described.

"Has he said anything?" Kenton asked.

Rachel shook her head. He hadn't, but she had seen the bank statements and the letter. Something was very wrong. And even if Jed did have problems with his current project, there's no way he'd make up the financial shortfall by returning to crime.

"I'll speak to him," she said.

"Make sure you do that. You know what it means if Jed is involved?"

Rachel nodded. "Me off the case." *And her life in tatters.*

"I wouldn't have much choice in the matter," Kenton said. "I'm prepared to give you a little longer to get the facts. If you're right and Jed is involved in this then I will become SIO and you will take a period of gardening leave until we know for sure the extent of what he's got himself into."

Great. Just what she needed.

CHAPTER TWENTY-ONE

After what Kenton had told her, Rachel had little appetite for work. The niggle about Jed was back. She returned to her own office and phoned Ray Hutton, arranging to speak to him at his home the following day. That done, she'd had enough. Rachel grabbed her things and left. She was aware of Elwyn watching her, a worried look on his face. What was the betting he'd ring her at home later? Hopefully, by then she'd have calmed down.

She was angry — with Jed for not confiding in her about his financial problems and with Kenton for jumping to conclusions.

It was the usual tortuous drive home. Too much traffic, no one giving an inch and a detour due to road works on the A6. Just what she needed on top of everything else. But for once, things were well organised at home. Jed had collected Len and was busy fixing a meal.

"Roast beef and all the trimmings." He smiled at her. "Thought you'd like a proper meal for once."

A nice idea, if only she'd been in the mood, but as it was, Rachel doubted she'd be able to eat a thing. She dumped her bag on the kitchen table and faced him. "We need to talk, Jed. I want the truth, not a load of lies you think'll make me feel better."

"Under arrest, am I?" He grinned. "Only if I am, I should tell you, I've done nowt, Officer."

His attitude irritated her. "You sure about that?"

He turned his attention from the hob and fixed his eyes on her. "What're you getting at? There's obviously something on your mind, so come on, spit it out."

"The Trio and their missing family members. Does that have anything to do with you?" She saw the surprise on his face. Was it because she'd asked the question or because she'd found him out?

"No, and to be honest, I'm shocked that you have to ask. I have no connection to my old life or the people I knew back then, Trio included. Where has this come from, Rachel?"

"I told you about Grace Blackmore's threats — that the Trio's family members must be returned, or our family would come to harm."

"So what? It's come to nothing, just as I suspected."

"Shut up and listen," she snapped at him. "The day after I told you about Grace's threat, the Agnew infant was found safe and well in a health centre. Don't you find that odd?"

"I imagine it'll have been a huge relief for his parents, but it's got nothing to do with me."

This was getting them nowhere. Jed parried every question with a feasible explanation, but she knew him, knew that look. He was lying. "You're in debt, you owe thousands we haven't got."

He turned his back on the cooker to face her. "You've been snooping."

"No, I haven't. You left your bank statements and that snotty letter from the bank manager lying around for any of us to find."

"No matter, it was never my intention to keep it secret. And they were business account statements, not my personal account. You're right, the business has problems. I've made some mistakes and they've proved costly." He shrugged and smiled at her. "Things will turn around. I have people putting it right as we speak."

"How d'you put right old mine workings, subsidence and contaminated land?"

Rachel saw the way his dark eyes narrowed. He looked both curious and angry at how the conversation was going.

"Someone's been telling tales. Who, Rachel?"

She didn't want to throw Kenton's name into the mix yet. "I can't say. Is it true? Is the land you've built on that bad?" Jed threw the tea towel he'd been holding onto the worktop and strode off towards the back door.

She followed him. "It is, isn't it? This time you've messed up completely. The McAteer magic has finally deserted you."

"I was misled," he threw back. "I've spent so long on the straight and narrow that I didn't spot the con in time."

Rachel shook her head. "You, conned? I don't believe it. Who would dare?"

"I was offered that tract of land cheap. It appeared perfect, close to the city centre and just what I was looking for to build forty affordable houses on."

"Sounds too good to be true to me."

"It was. I know that now. A firm of solicitors handled the legal stuff. They told me the seller was abroad and that he needed the cash and wanted the deal to go through ultra-quick. I should have twigged then, realised there was something wrong. Two days later the solicitor turned up at my office with the signed contract in his hand. If I wanted the land, it was now or never. I'd been to the site, even took a surveyor with me. He said the place looked sound. I should have waited for the searches to come back, but I didn't. An expensive mistake." He went out and sat on the garden seat. "I broke all the rules, Rachel. I paid cash and didn't do the checks. I was offered that land on the cheap. My hand was forced, I needed to act swiftly. I was conned."

"Who signed the contract?"

"A James Smith, the owner. A man of that name did own the land, I checked with the land registry."

"D'you know him?" she asked.

"No. I've asked around, and neither does anyone else, but it's a common enough name. When I found out about the problems with the land, I went back to the solicitor, but he refused to help. Said there was nothing he could do, the deal was done, money had changed hands and the seller was now uncontactable."

Now it was Rachel's turn to be confused. "What about planning permission? Surely the council must know about the land."

"I didn't submit the plans until after I'd bought it. When I did contact the council, I got permission for half the number of houses, those on the east side of the land. All well and good, but the problems keep on coming."

"Do you know who did this to you? Who's really behind setting you up?"

He shook his head. "Not a clue."

"The Trio?"

"Possibly, but I don't understand why they'd bother. Nor do I know what's happened to their family members. That kid really was missing, I take it?"

"Yes, Louise Agnew wasn't acting, all that emotion was genuine. Mind you, her husband didn't appear as bothered as he should have been." She frowned. "You should have told me all this before, Jed. This is no time to keep things back."

"Someone wanted me to buy that land. They wanted it to cripple me financially. I was warned by a friend that it was a con, but I took no notice. All I could see was the houses I wanted to build and the profit I would make."

"Which friend?"

"An old mate of mine, a solicitor who at one time wasn't averse to taking a hefty bribe but who, like me, has been on the straight and narrow for a while. These days he's big time, charges the earth for his services. I should have listened to him, it would have saved me a packet."

"Do I know him?"

"You might, but his name won't have come up recently, Nigel Fortune, or Nidge as he's known."

CHAPTER TWENTY-TWO

Joe felt bad about his last conversation with Lee, but he couldn't do with her constant fussing. He'd arranged to meet a dealer in the gardens later, someone who owed him. Hiding away like Lee wanted wouldn't get him the fix he needed.

He sat with the others in the alley, killing time. Sponger, his mate, had a bag of sandwiches from the soup kitchen and was quite happily handing them around.

"Get you anything, I can," he boasted. "Smile nicely, put on that 'little boy lost' look and Dora's a pushover."

Joe gave a nod. The lad wasn't nicknamed 'Sponger' for nothing.

"What're you up to then?" Sponger asked.

"Got a meet later, after that, who knows?"

"What's happened to that bird you used to hang around with? A looker, she is."

Joe frowned. Why had he asked that? Sponger wasn't usually so interested in his friends. "Don't know, think she must have done one."

"Well, I'm off too. Going to queue at the hostel. I can't sleep out tonight, my back's killing me."

Joe gave Sponger a nod and turned up the collar on his jacket. It was getting dark, cold too. He pulled the waterproof Lee had left around him. It would be a long night.

Joe nodded off. He didn't know how long he'd been asleep but when he woke, the others had gone. He was sitting on the concrete slabs leaning against the wall. His legs were so stiff that he could barely move them. He tried to stand and groaned at the pain.

"Did a good job from the look of things, the gang that crippled you. Left you in a right bad way."

Joe didn't recognise the voice. He looked up to see a man dressed in dark clothing standing over him. He looked scary enough, but what really terrified Joe was the baseball bat he had in his hand.

"Reckon they must have used something like this." He bent over and looked in Joe's eyes. "Right, aren't I?"

Joe was shaking. "What d'you want?"

"Lee. Where is she?"

This had to be the man Lee had got involved with, the one she was so scared of. "Gone. Earlier today she got her stuff together and walked off. I don't think she'll be back."

"You can do better than that." The man tapped his other hand with the bat. "You have to. Your life depends on it."

Joe struggled to get to his feet. If he could only reach the entrance to the alley someone might see what was happening and help him. "Look, we weren't that close, and anyway she never told anyone her plans."

The first blow hit Joe on his shoulder. The second caught him across his temple. Joe slumped to one side, stunned. For a moment he thought his skull was split.

"Better you talk to me, Joe. Save yourself a lot of pain."

"I can't. I don't know anything. Really."

The man sighed and then suddenly struck the wall with the bat. The loud 'thwack' resounded in the alley. "Be warned, Joe. I can do real damage with this. What's it to be?"

"Please! Lee never said where she was going. If I knew, I'd say."

The man leaned in closer again. "You're lying. Well, I'm going to make you talk."

The blows rained down on Joe's body for what seemed like an eternity. When they finally stopped, he was lying face down in the alley with blood on his hands. Then he heard a clunk as the man threw the bat onto the concrete slabs. For a second, he dared to hope that it was over. But when he looked up, he saw that his attacker had traded the bat for a knife, a wicked-looking thing that made Joe shudder.

The man flipped Joe onto his back and straddled his body. "You could have made it easier for us both," he said. "All you had to do was speak to me, tell me where Lee's gone." He gripped Joe's chin, forcing his head round to face him. "I didn't want to do this, but you give me no choice." He drew the blade down Joe's right cheek. "Blood, Joe. Your face looks a right mess."

Joe stared up, his eyes wide, as the man waved the blade in front of his face. It was mesmerising, like a pendulum, and Joe felt sick. There wasn't a single place on his body that didn't hurt. He coughed and spat out a mouthful of blood.

"I have to go," his attacker said. "Pity, I was just starting to enjoy myself." He gave no warning of what was coming next. He grasped Joe's chin and tipped his head back, smiled one last time into Joe's terrified eyes and with one deft stroke, slit his throat from ear to ear.

CHAPTER TWENTY-THREE

Day Four: Wednesday

The next morning, Rachel woke refreshed. Despite her worries about Jed, his business and whether he was involved in her current case, she'd fallen asleep exhausted and slept the night through. Jed saw to Len, leaving Rachel free to catch up on much needed sleep. She woke feeling more human and decided to make an effort — wear her new jacket and fix her hair. Despite being all fired up when she'd arrived home the previous evening, the chat with Jed and what he'd told her made her feel better, his explanation rang true. What would have been unthinkable a few years ago had happened, and he'd been set up. No wonder he was preoccupied.

Giving him a peck on the cheek, she made for the door. "I'll be back for tea. Len goes to nursery this morning and he needs picking up at one." She knew Jed was fine with the arrangement, he was going to work from home today.

"I'll speak to the bank," he said as she left. "I'm confident they'll extend the overdraft and then I'll have the project back on track in no time."

Rachel could only hope he was right. She didn't want to see everything Jed had worked for go down the pan. Problems at home or not, she'd have to shelve them for now. Work was far too busy.

She decided to see Hutton before checking in at the station. It was on the way, in the Stockport suburb of Cheadle. It was a modest house, unlike Grace's splendid mansion, an average-size detached on an estate of similar properties, and Hutton himself was nothing like Rachel had imagined. Grace Blackmore and Scott Agnew were both in their mid-fifties, Hutton was early forties tops. He was tall and well built, as if he worked out regularly.

"Please tell me you've got some news," he said, as soon as Rachel had introduced herself.

"Nothing yet, Mr Hutton. We have her on CCTV being wheeled to the car but nothing after that. Whoever took her knew the area, down to the roads with CCTV. He was clever."

"I don't understand how anyone could take an old lady like her. She's fragile, lives in a care home and needs routine. It's inhumane."

"If we find anything, hear a rumour, or get any information at all, we'll be on it. Take heart from the fact that little James Agnew was returned unharmed."

"I keep reminding myself of that. I'm pleased for Scott and Louise of course, but there's a big difference between an infant and a grown woman who will be able to tell people exactly what happened to her."

Rachel gave him her card. "Anything changes — a phone call, anything, give me a ring." She left him standing on the doorstep looking despondent.

* * *

She had just passed Stockport when she got the call from Elwyn.

"We've got a body, a young lad found in an alley off Oldham Road in the city centre."

Rachel groaned. As if they didn't have enough on with the Trio's missing family members. "Suspicious death?"

"Very much so, Rachel. He's been badly beaten and whoever did it finished off by slitting his throat. He was found early this morning by a bloke heading for work. Tent's up and the area's been cordoned off."

"Any clue as to who he is?"

"No, but he could be a rough sleeper. He's got that look — you know, half-starved, well-worn clothing and dirty."

This would put extra pressure on the team, resources would be tight, but it couldn't be helped. "I'll meet you there, text me the postcode."

* * *

Jude was already there when Rachel arrived. The forensic scientist was busy examining and bagging a number of items strewn on the ground. She looked up and smiled at her friend. "I'm guessing he's another of this city's homeless. His clothing and other stuff is littering the alleyway."

"Rough sleeper, you say. Any similarities to the girl from the other week?"

"I'm not sure yet, but the method of killing was the same, beating and then the throat slit. Colin will be able to tell you more once he's done the PM."

Rachel stuck her head around the tent flap. A gruesome sight, there was so much blood it was difficult to make out a face. Elwyn was talking to Colin Butterworth, the pathologist.

"Watch your step," Elwyn warned her. "I'd say he was killed here. There's a lot of blood and his belongings are all scattered around this spot."

"Looks that way," Rachel said. "Poor sod, they smashed him up with something hard before finishing him off with the knife. His right arm is badly broken. Hand too." She took a closer look at the body. He was young, possibly in his late teens or early twenties, skinny, and his clothing was dirty and ripped. It looked as if Jude was right, a rough sleeper. "Anything on him to help ID him?"

"Not that I know of, only the sleeping bag and the odd bits of clothing Jude is picking up," Elwyn said.

Rachel leaned forward to get a better look at his face. "He's been bashed about and is very bloody, but he looks familiar to me. How about you, Elwyn?"

"I'm not sure. Perhaps when he's been cleaned up a bit back at the morgue."

Rachel was remembering someone from a few months ago, a young man and a puzzle that had never been resolved. "Imagine him tall and straight, with clean clothes and fast on his feet."

"You know him?" he asked.

"I'm not sure, but there is something." Rachel stared at his legs and feet. "It's him, Elwyn, I know it is."

"Who, Rachel?"

"Take a good look at those trainers, Elwyn. They're old and battered now but when I first saw this lad, they were new, a vivid yellow with red stripes."

"They're very distinctive, I'll give you that." He looked puzzled.

"I told you about him at the time. In fact, you said you were going to find out more for me."

He'd obviously forgotten.

"Cast your mind back to the last big case we worked on before I went off on maternity leave. This is the young lad who collared me in the street a couple of times and told me my parents' death was no accident."

CHAPTER TWENTY-FOUR

"Unknown male found murdered in an alley off Oldham Road. Beaten and throat cut," Rachel told the team back at the station. "First priority is to give him a name. Jude has taken a number of items back to the lab. With luck, she'll have something soon."

"It looks highly likely that he was a rough sleeper," Elwyn added. "That means in all probability missing persons is unlikely to be much help. We've no idea how long he's been out there."

"Elwyn's right." Rachel looked at Jonny Farrell. "You've got contacts among the people who help the homeless in the city. Go and see them, take a photo of the dead lad and see what you can turn up."

"I'll do the rounds and call in at the hostels. Someone might know him."

"Amy, you carry on with your investigations into the Trio. Anything juicy, let me know at once." She gestured for Elwyn to join her in her office.

"The lad found in the alley, still got the CCTV from when he spoke to me a few months ago?" she asked.

"Filed away with the other stuff from that case."

"Will you dig it out? We'll have another look. I'll speak to Nell Hennessey too." She thought for a moment, trying to recall what was said at the time. "She warned me off, I remember that, but not officially. She said the lad was mixed up in another case."

"She might be helpful, but Nell has a lot on her plate these days what with her mother."

Rachel nodded. I'll ring her this morning. I want to know what she didn't tell me back then. Details of the case our victim was involved in will do for starters."

Rachel already had Nell's number on her mobile and rang her as soon as Elwyn had gone back to the main office. Pleasantries over, she got straight to the point. "I could do with a word. We've got the body of a young man in the morgue, brutally murdered, and we need to identify him."

"You think I can help?" Nell sounded surprised.

"I have a photo. All I want you to do is look at it and see if you recognise him."

"I'll do my best but I'm not on the ball like I used to be. Caring for Dee, my mother, has knocked the edge off. Half the time I don't know what bloody day it is. But if it's impor- tant, come round, I'll make you a cuppa and you can ask your questions. Dee goes to the local day centre today, so I'm here alone. I had to move to a more comfortable place for Dee, so I'm living in Stockport now. I'll text you the address."

Rachel had no idea why Nell always called her mother by her first name and she'd never asked, but there had to be a story there. "See you within the hour," Rachel said.

* * *

Nell Hennessey's new address was a huge, detached house in Heaton Norris. It had a large garden and was set well back off the busy road. The ex-DCI had retired in style.

She greeted Rachel with a smile and apologised for the mess. "I'm having work done, a couple of rooms converted to make life easier for Dee. It's not going to be long before she needs constant care. I intend to ensure she has every comfort. Once the house is finished, I'll hire a live-in nurse for her."

Rachel looked around — expensive house, not to mention the furniture and fittings. This little lot must have cost a fortune.

"Round-the-clock care. You must be dreading the expense," Rachel said.

"I am, but the nurse will be a godsend. She's met Dee and they get on. That's half the battle." She smiled. "It'll cost a bit, but I want her happy and that means keeping Dee at home with me."

Rachel was aware that the cost of a decent nursing home was eye-watering, but a live-in nurse would be even more costly. Nell had been a DCI like her, she'd have a good pension but the money to pay for a house like this and the care she spoke of took some finding.

Nell must have sensed Rachel's curiosity. "My aunt, Dee's sister, died five years ago. She looked after me for several years when I was a kid. Diane had no children of her own, so she left me her property in Oxfordshire to help with the costs she knew would inevitably arise. Until I retired, I rented the place out but with property prices rising, that house turned out to be worth a packet. I sold the place and used the money to pay for all this."

Rachel laughed. "And there was me thinking you'd robbed a bank."

"Had Diane not been so generous I might have had to," Nell said. "I couldn't bear the thought of Dee being stuck somewhere she didn't like."

Nell walked into the kitchen and switched the kettle on. "So, what can I do for you?"

Rachel took her mobile from her pocket and showed Nell the photo of the dead man. "He met a brutal end and we've yet to find out who he is. D'you know him?"

Nell took a good look. She handed back the phone with a shake of her head. "What makes you think I do?"

"His trainers," Rachel said. "He's the young man who ran up to me in the street a few months ago and said the death of my parents was no accident. Remember, I told you about it at the time."

Nell placed two mugs on the worktop. She cleared her throat. "Are you sure about that? It was quite a while ago."

But Rachel had seen the look on her face. Nell did recognise him. "It's him all right," she said.

"I'm still not sure I can be much help."

"You told me to leave it, that this man was part of another investigation," Rachel said.

"Look, Rachel, perhaps I did, but months have passed since then and like you, I've got plenty of other stuff to think about." Her tone was snippy. Nell obviously didn't like the way this was going.

"Surely you can recall what the investigation was about, who it involved? I got the impression it was big."

Nell handed Rachel a mug and gestured for her to sit down at the table. "I was told not to talk about it."

Rachel tapped the image. "Look, Nell, I need a name. His family should know what's happened to him. Apart from that, I want to know the truth about my parents' death."

Nell took a sip of her tea. "Who are you chasing?"

"The Trio. Someone is targeting them. We think it's a takeover, but who knows? Any information you have about this young man could help us."

Nell looked surprised. "The Trio, eh? Be careful, Rachel. They get wind you're after them and you'll become a target yourself."

"It's complicated, Nell. So far, we've got two, possibly three dead youngsters and suspect that the Trio are involved somewhere."

"We were a very small part of an investigation into organised crime in Manchester," Nell said after a pause. "That's all I know. Two weeks in our station was suddenly pulled. We were told not to talk about what we'd been doing."

"Organised crime? D'you mean the Trio?"

"I don't know, we never got that far."

"Do you know the lad's name?"

"Joe Collins," Nell said finally. "He gave us some information about a robbery, as I recall."

That was all very well but that didn't explain how he knew about Rachel's parents. "How come he knew my mum and dad?"

"I don't know why he approached you, Rachel. Whatever reason he had for doing so is lost on me."

CHAPTER TWENTY-FIVE

Up until Joe Collins had approached her, Rachel hadn't suspected for a moment that there was anything suspicious about her parents' death. Now she had no idea what to believe.

Rachel headed back to the station. She'd speak to Elwyn, tell him about Collins, see what he thought. She was heading down the A6 towards Ardwick when her mobile rang. It was Jude.

"I've found something among the dead man's belongings I collected."

"I know his name if that's what it is," Rachel said.

"So do we — Joe Collins. His prints are on the system. He was brought in with a dealer a while back, spent a night in the cells. But that's not why I'm ringing. Among the clothing I picked up was a waterproof jacket. I could tell from the size that it wasn't Joe's — too small. In one of the pockets I found an old purse. There was no money in it but a label inside read 'Leona Lomax.'"

"Isn't she the sister of the dead girl you spoke about?" Rachel asked.

"Yes. It looks as if the girls must have known Joe, maybe they even went around together. Laura and Joe are dead, both murdered. It's possible that Leona is in danger too. You need to find her quickly."

Rachel sighed. If only it was that easy. They had no clue what the girl even looked like, but then she had an idea. "Jude, when she spoke to you about Laura, was she within shot of the CCTV cameras?"

"It's possible. She sat in the corridor waiting and there is a camera there. I'll check."

"If you get an image of her, text it to me. I'll put Jonny on the job."

* * *

Back at the station, Rachel asked Elwyn to come into her office for a word. Amy was nowhere to be seen and Jonny had left a note on his desk to say he'd gone to the soup kitchen. She'd text him about Leona if Jude found that image.

"Nell wasn't very informative," Rachel began. "She reckons she knows nothing about my parents' death or what the lad, Joe Collins, wanted to tell me."

Elwyn smiled. "You don't look convinced."

"I'm not. Don't ask me why, but I got the feeling Nell wasn't telling me the truth. Call it instinct, but she was lying, I just know it."

Elwyn looked doubtful. "Why would she do that, Rachel? Nell has no reason to lie to you."

Rachel wasn't so sure. Nell's story of the inheritance hadn't rung true either. It was the way she'd avoided her eyes when she'd told her about it.

"Since retiring, Nell's bought a huge house and is about to hire a full-time live-in nurse for her mum. She told me her mum's sister had left them some money, but I don't think that's true."

"What good would that serve? You're suggesting Nell has something to hide? You can't really believe that, Rachel. I worked with the woman, I thought she was straight as a die."

"Okay, but do something for me," she said. "Check out the money. Find out if Nell really did inherit a large amount."

Elwyn didn't look too sure. "I'll check the probate records. That'll give me the details."

"Nell's mum is called Dee Hennessey and her sister was Diane. Track back from there. Find out if Diane owned any property at all for starters."

Elwyn sighed. "Keep it to myself?"

"Please. Let's see what you turn up before I decide what to do."

"It's a dangerous game, Rachel. You've admitted yourself that all you have to go on is your instinct."

"It doesn't usually fail me."

Elwyn shrugged. "Get anything else?"

"We now have a name for the dead lad. Leona was his friend, it's vital we find her before the people working for the Trio do. She'll have information that we can use. We should also try and find any family he may have had."

"If she's any sense, this Leona will be aware of that and have gone into hiding."

"Did you get that footage for me?" Rachel asked.

Elwyn put a USB stick on her desk. "It's all on there."

"Thanks, I'll look at it later." Rachel's mobile pinged. Jude had sent the photo of Leona. She held it up for Elwyn to see. "This is her. I'll send it to Jonny, he's out on the streets asking about Joe. With luck he'll find someone who will tell him where she is."

"She knows the lad, Joe, and the dead girl, Laura, is her sister. Ask yourself, Rachel. What part has she played in all this?" Elwyn said.

"What d'you mean?"

"The girl in the image has short blonde hair, so did the girl who abducted Edith Hutton. I know the photo we've got from the home is only a back view but the hair, body shape and height are the same."

Elwyn was right. Suddenly it hit Rachel. "Stupid girl, she's trying to get even. She can't hope to manage that on her own. She's one girl against the Trio."

"She might have help. She could be working for whoever is attempting the suspected takeover."

"If Grace Blackmore gets hold of her, Leona will be dead meat."

CHAPTER TWENTY-SIX

Having once worked with the people helping the homeless on Manchester's streets, DC Jonny Farrell was familiar with the hostels and soup kitchens and had a contact by the name of Terry who worked nights dishing out food and warm clothing. That afternoon he made for a hostel off Bloom Street in the city centre. The current manager was a woman called Dora.

Dora was mopping the floor ready for opening up later. She was happy to talk but doubted she could give him much help.

He showed her the image of Joe Collins. "What about this lad? Seen him around?"

Dora stopped mopping and studied the photo. "Had an accident, has he? Only he don't look well."

He gave her a half-hearted smile that soon faded. "This is the only one we've got. It was taken in the morgue. You see, Joe was murdered. We suspect he was living on the streets and we're trying to find out a bit about him. Who he went around with, who his friends were."

"If he were living rough, he won't have had many friends, love. It's hard out there and no one gives a toss about anyone else. All most of them are bothered about is getting their next fix."

"But have you seen him in here?" he said.

"I might have done. I can't be sure."

Jonny showed her the photo of Leona which Rachel had sent him. "What about her?"

Dora smiled. "That's Lee, I think her proper name is Leona. That's where I've seen him, I remember now. She and the lad went about together for a while, but I haven't seen either of them recently."

"Is there anything you can tell me about them?"

"Lee was a quiet one. She kept her head down, you know, didn't like attention. But she had money, I remember that. Came in here and was happy to pay for the pair of them. At one time she had a sister in tow, pretty girl but younger. I haven't seen her in weeks either."

Happy to chat she might be, but Dora wasn't giving him anything new. "Is Terry working later?"

"He'll be on th'streets with the food as usual. You'll find him about ten tonight in Piccadilly Gardens. D'you know him then?"

"Yes, he's helped me before on another case."

"Canny lad is our Terry. If those young 'uns have been hanging around the street for any length of time, he'll know them."

Jonny thanked her and made his way back to the car park. There wasn't much he could do until later. In the meantime he'd go back to the station and tell the team what he was up to. He'd speak to Terry later.

* * *

When Jonny got back, Rachel and Elwyn were in the canteen getting some food. Amy was at her desk pushing pieces of paper around.

"I'm sick of this. I get all the pedestrian stuff shoved on my plate. I know why she does it, stupid bitch is jealous. The sooner I move up and on the better."

Jonny tutted. "Rachel knows what she's doing, Amy. We all do our bit with the research."

"Not you, I notice."

"I'm only out today because of the contacts I made on another case. Take over if you think you can do better," he said.

Amy smiled up at him. "Not a bad idea, what you up to next then?"

"Hanging around Piccadilly Gardens tonight, waiting for a bloke called Terry."

Amy's face fell. "Can't tonight, I'm having dinner with Mark. We're going to that new Spanish place on Deansgate."

He smiled. "That's why Rachel gives you the research. She knows you too well."

Amy glared at the computer screen and swore. "I hate this job, d'you know that?"

"Have you got anything on the Trio yet?" he asked.

"No chance. Nothing these last three years and before then not much either. On the surface they're model citizens."

Jonny sat down at his desk and fired up his computer. "I'll give you a hand if you like," he called over to Amy. "Who d'you want me to look at?"

"Agnew is the most interesting," she said. "He's been married before and has three grown-up children. They all live away and none of them have a social media presence."

"Warned off by their father perhaps?" Jonny wondered.

"Who knows, not me and I don't much fancy finding out either. In fact, I'm going to call it a day and go home early," Amy decided.

"Rachel won't like it. She's expecting progress."

"She can do one."

Amy was all set to leave when the office phone rang. It was the duty sergeant asking to speak to Rachel. When the call finished, Amy turned to Jonny, suddenly pale. "We've got a problem. And DCI King isn't going to like it."

"Why, what's happened?"

"Another body. Butterworth and the CSI team are already on it."

"Do we know who it is?" Jonny asked.

"Yes, and that's the problem. It's Brendan Blackmore."

"The man's been missing for days. Given the problems the Trio are having, I doubt DCI King will be that surprised."

"Thing is, Jonny, he's been found on a building site belonging to Jed McAteer."

CHAPTER TWENTY-SEVEN

Liam tried but couldn't find anything useful to help Lee. There was nothing on any of the dodgy sites he used about Ronzo or anyone else working against the Trio. But he did discover that Joe was dead. "He was beaten to death, Lee. You know what that means. If he knew anything about your whereabouts, he'll have told them."

The news upset Lee and it also made her nervous. Joe had no idea where she'd gone so couldn't have told them anything. Even so, knowing Ronzo was still on her tail worried her. She should have tried harder to help Joe, insist he went into hiding too. Lee stared out of the window at the gardens belonging to the student living complex and beyond, to Oxford Road. Liam was right. Right now there could be anyone out there just waiting for her to show her face. "I should have made Joe listen to me. He didn't understand the danger. I should have spelled it out, made him run while he had the chance."

"My advice for what it's worth is go to the police. Tell them what you know and ask them for help."

That was the last thing Lee wanted to do. They were more likely to lock her up, never mind help her. "I kidnapped a kid and an old woman, the only thing they'll do is charge me."

"The kid has been returned," he said.

"What about Edith? Have you found anything on her whereabouts?"

"Nothing."

"There you are then. For all we know she could be dead, and if she is that makes me party to murder."

Liam shook his head. "You didn't know what would happen to her. You have information, the police will do a deal. Tell them you were forced to do those things."

"But I wasn't. Ronzo offered me the chance to get even, and I took it. I wanted to get back at them where it hurt the most. And I didn't return the kid. That must have been down to Ronzo."

"You can't sort this on your own, Lee."

He was right on that score. Not only that, the longer she stayed with Liam the more danger she put him in. Decision made. "I'll go. Ronzo finds me here he'll kill you too."

"Ring the police, Lee," Liam urged her. "There's a detective running the case, Rachel King. Speak to her."

"How d'you know that?"

He gave her a cheeky grin and nodded at his laptop. "There's lots of things I shouldn't know but do. She's based at East Manchester. Ring the station, they'll put you through."

"Joe told me about her a while ago. I'll think about it." She grabbed her rucksack. "For now, I'll leave you in peace."

Liam had been a real friend when she'd needed one, but she couldn't keep imposing on his good nature. She had to get away. Lee changed into her dark clothing in the shower block and pulled up the hood on her top to cover her distinctive blonde hair. She hoped to make her escape among the students outside and take the back streets to Piccadilly station. There, she'd get on a train going north. Lee had a friend from school who'd moved to Scotland who was always banging on about wanting to see her.

Head down and walking at a steady pace so as not to draw attention to herself, Lee ventured out. It was a pleasant day, the warmth of the sunshine cheered her up. It was sad about Joe but there was nothing she could do about him now. She had to save herself. She crossed Oxford Street and was on Grosvenor Street when she saw it, a silver car going at a snail's pace. It was following her.

"Get in," Ronzo barked.

Lee was terrified. If Ronzo got hold of her, she wouldn't last the day. She tore along the footpath away from the car and darted down an alley with bollards blocking the entrance. She'd escaped for now but that did nothing to ease her terror. She ran to the end of the alley and turned onto the road leading to the station. A glance to her left and she saw the car again. This wasn't going to work. There was no way she could outrun them.

"You're trying my patience, Lee," Ronzo shouted at her. "Now get in the car."

Lee had stopped momentarily to catch her breath. "No! Leave me alone. I want nothing more to do with you."

Ronzo laughed. "Too late. You know too much."

"Are these men bothering you, love?"

Lee spun round to see a burly bloke in a tracksuit standing behind her. Her mouth too dry to speak, she nodded.

The stranger bent forward and said something to Ronzo, who drove off at speed. "I told him I'm a police constable from Central. Which I am. My car's parked round the corner, can I drop you somewhere?"

It was a narrow escape. Without the stranger's intervention, Ronzo would have dragged her into the car, and she would no doubt have suffered the same fate as Laura and Joe. However much she might fear what the police might do to her, it was nothing in comparison to that.

"I need to see a DCI King at East Manchester nick. I need to speak to her. She can help me."

* * *

Rachel and Elwyn were on their way back to the main office when Rachel's mobile rang. It was Kenton.

"I need to talk to you now, we have a problem."

Rachel sighed and turned to Elwyn. "Kenton's fretting again. I'll dump my bag and go and see what he wants."

They got to the office to find no sign of Amy. Jonny was on the phone. Call over, he turned to the pair. "A sergeant from Central is on his way over with Leona Lomax. She came out of hiding and was chased. She walked into Central and asked to see you. The girl's scared and wants to talk. She's heard about Joe Collins and reckons she's next."

"I think she's right," Rachel said. "When she arrives, you and Elwyn look after her. When I've seen what Kenton wants, we'll interview her."

She left them to it and went along the corridor to see Kenton. He was shuffling paperwork around, but Rachel could tell his mind wasn't on it. "Sit down," he said. "Brendan Blackmore is dead."

Straight to the point but given how long he'd been missing it didn't surprise her. "What happened? How did he die — natural causes or was he murdered?"

"Butterworth is at the scene. When he's done his stuff, we'll know more about what happened."

"I should go, see for myself."

"No, Rachel, you must not get involved," Kenton said firmly. "Blackmore was found on a building site belonging to Jed. If there is any suspicion of foul play, you must leave everything to your team. I'll take over. I'll work with DS Pryce."

For a second, Rachel thought this was some sick joke, but Kenton's face said otherwise. "Which . . . which site?"

"The one giving him all the trouble. The body has been there for several days."

"In that case, Blackmore met his end before the Agnew infant and Edith Hutton were taken," she said.

"We'll need confirmation on time of death, but it looks that way."

"It can't have anything to do with Jed," she insisted. "There's no way he'd get involved in murder."

"Easy to say, Rachel, but I'll still have to speak to him, ask if he's had any dealings with Blackmore recently."

"He hasn't, we've already had that little chat."

"If Blackmore was murdered, we'll need more than just Jed's word," he said. "I'm not happy about any of this. My instincts tell me I should haul Jed in for a formal interview and take you off the case."

"What would that achieve, Mark?" she asked angrily. "It might ease your conscience to do things by the book but consider what's more important, collaring Jed or finding out who really killed Blackmore."

"I've bent the rules as it is, but for now we won't make assumptions about how he died. Butterworth and Forensics will do their bit. Once we have the report and know more about how Blackmore was killed I want you to take a back seat, Rachel. Do you understand?"

She nodded. There was no way she'd win this one. "I'm still on the case but not able to do my job properly, great," she said wearily. "We've had a call from a girl called Leona Lomax. We believe she's the kidnapper. I need to interview her."

"She's connected to the case, so get someone else to speak to her. I mean it, Rachel. For now, you stay well away from it."

CHAPTER TWENTY-EIGHT

It was late afternoon by the time Rachel left Kenton's office. Elwyn had put Leona in one of the interview rooms. As she couldn't be part of it, he would have to interview her, but she would watch, listen closely to what the girl said.

Her mobile rang. It was Jed. "Where are you?" she asked.

"At home, looking after Len," he said. "I've had a call from your nick. Kenton wants me to come in for a chat. Blackmore's been found on my site — dead."

"I know. Kenton's just told me. I'm not happy, Jed. It means I'm off the case and you'll have to be interviewed."

"Surely Kenton doesn't think I had anything to do with Blackmore's death?" He sounded surprised.

"We don't know how he died yet, but I'm praying it was an accident."

"That'll mean health and safety breathing down my neck for the foreseeable."

A small price to pay in Rachel's opinion. "Not funny, Jed. The man's dead and was found on your property. When Kenton speaks to you, make sure you tell him the truth, whatever that is." Rachel finished the call. She'd speak to Jed at home when the interview with Leona was over. She'd hang around long enough to have a quick word with Elwyn afterwards and then call it a day.

Rachel didn't have long to wait. Loud voices on the corridor alerted her to an argument. She went out to see what was going on. Jonny was rubbing his cheek.

"The little madam punched me one," he said indignantly.

"You wound me up," Leona retorted. "I'm here because I need protecting not because I'm guilty of anything." She looked at Rachel. "This idiot wants my fingerprints and DNA."

"You're Leona?"

"The girl nodded. "I prefer Lee."

"Okay, Lee. You're here because you are in danger and can give us information that might prove useful. There is also the matter of the abductions, a serious crime that carries a heavy penalty."

"Are you threatening me? Is this a matter of I talk or you throw the book at me?"

"You need to calm down, for now it's just about procedure. When that's sorted, DS Pryce and DC Farrell will interview you."

"No."

"You came to us, Lee, said you wanted to help, and in return we'll keep you safe."

"And I will help. But I want to talk to *you*, not this pair of clowns."

Rachel looked at the two men and shook her head. "Elwyn — a word. Jonny, sit with Lee. I won't be long."

Rachel walked towards the main office, Elwyn following in her wake.

"Blackmore's been found dead on one of Jed's sites," she told him. "So, naturally Kenton wants me off the case. I have told him about Leona but he's adamant."

"She's asked for you. The girl is stubborn, Rachel. We can't afford to have her clam up."

Kenton was standing in the doorway. "Who's that young woman sounding off in the interview room? I can hear her from my office."

"Leona Lomax, sir," Elwyn said. "She's asked for help. There's every possibility that she knows the people attempting to take over from the Trio, but she's insisting on only speaking to DCI King."

Kenton's face fell. "Do you know this young woman?" he asked Rachel.

"No, but I have some background on her and a probable motive for why she was out to get the Trio."

"I'll speak to her first."

* * *

When Kenton joined Lee and Jonny in the interview room, Lee was pacing with her arms folded.

"You're not Rachel King," she said to him. "It's her, or I'll take my chances."

"Why?"

"Because she's been in this from the beginning," Lee replied.

"Have you heard the name Blackmore during your recent activities?" Kenton asked.

"Yes, but I've had nowt to do with him, only Agnew and Hutton."

"You've never met Blackmore?"

She glared at him. "No, I told you. I know who he is, but our paths have never crossed."

"And if they had?"

"I'd have done my best to hurt him," she spat and plonked herself down in a chair. "I'm not saying anything else until you fetch DCI King. Then I'll tell you what I know about the Trio and the lot that's trying to wreck their perfect little lives."

CHAPTER TWENTY-NINE

Kenton escorted Rachel to the interview room. "We don't appear to have much choice. You and Pryce do this, but don't push it. I'll be watching, so keep it strictly about Agnew and Hutton."

"What about the murder of her sister and Joe Collins? She could have important information about them too," Rachel said.

"Just don't get onto the subject of Blackmore, and if she mentions Jed's name, you're out of there. Do you understand? Her evidence could prove to be important, and I won't have your personal involvement jeopardising the case further down the line."

Rachel agreed. What choice did she have? She and Elwyn went in and sat down opposite Lee and the duty solicitor.

Lee nodded at him. "Is he really needed? I'm here to help, cut a deal, I don't expect to get locked up, so why do I need a lawyer?"

"He's here to advise you, Lee," Rachel said. "Now, tell us what prompted you to come here today."

"Because I'm shit scared, simple as that. There are people out there who want me dead," Lee said. "I got into something too deep. I've seen at least one of them. I can describe him. I know stuff, and that's dangerous."

"Do these people have names?" Rachel asked.

"I only ever met one of them to talk to but there are others. The man who was after me in the car today is called Ronzo."

"D'you know his full name?"

"No."

"D'you know anyone else who's involved?"

"Ronzo, the man I dealt with, spoke of a boss, a woman, although he never said what her name was."

"You're sure about that? The person attempting a take-over from the Trio is a *woman*?" Rachel exclaimed. If this was the case, it meant Jed was out of the picture.

"Well, I never met her, but he referred to the boss as 'her' more than once."

"This Ronzo, that his surname?" Elwyn asked.

Lee shook her head. "Not sure, could be."

"How did they find you?" Rachel asked.

"Through Joe. I was angry after what happened to my sister, Laura. I don't deny it, I wanted revenge. I wanted to kill whoever was responsible, make them suffer. Next thing I know Joe's speaking to people about me, then he gets this call — Ronzo wanting to meet me. He was just what I was looking for, a way to get to the bastards who murdered my sister."

"It was you kidnapped the Agnew infant?" Elwyn asked.

Lee looked at each officer in turn. "I say yes and you've got me. Like you said, kidnap is a serious crime. You could lock me up and throw away the key."

"Except that we want your help, Lee. As I see it there is a deal to be done."

The girl appeared to think about this. "Yes, I took the kid. Not what I wanted but it was a way of getting back at Scott Agnew. Ronzo saw to all the background stuff, the babysitting service, the identity badge and that. All I had to do was turn up, sit with the kid a while then take him to Ronzo, who was waiting outside in a car."

Rachel's eyes narrowed. How could she do something like that to an innocent? "Weren't you concerned about what would happen to this baby?"

Lee shrugged. "A little, but I wanted the Agnews to suffer, know what it was like to lose someone they loved, like I had."

"The child was returned unharmed," Rachel told her. Lee looked surprised. "A tall, well-built man left him at a health centre. Does that description fit Ronzo?"

"No. He wasn't much taller than me I'd say, and medium built."

"Ronzo caught up with you today. Tell me what happened."

"I left my mate's place on Oxford Road making for Piccadilly station. Next thing I'm being chased down Grosvenor Street by Ronzo in a car."

Rachel nodded to a uniformed officer in the room with them. "Get on to traffic for the CCTV, we'll have a look."

"What did they do to Joe?" Lee asked.

"Beaten, stabbed and left in an alley off Oldham Road," Elwyn said.

"I warned him. I told Joe to hide. Ronzo rang me, threatened to kill him if I didn't show myself."

"You should have contacted us then," Rachel said. "How did you know it was me leading the case?"

"A friend I've been staying with found out, but Joe mentioned you as well. You met him a while ago, before he got beaten the first time. Back then he was sharp, and he could run too."

"I remember him," Rachel said. "He spoke to me a couple of times. Ran up to me in the street with some tale about my parents."

"I know. He told me about it."

Rachel leaned forward. "D'you know what he wanted to tell me?"

"He felt bad about what happened to them. He told me it was a case of wrong place, wrong time, that's what got them killed. Your father was a barrister."

Rachel nodded.

"Your parents were at a service station after leaving the M56. Your dad saw a group of three people talking on the forecourt, one of them a high-ranking detective who he knew from his work. The cop was talking to two men — a known dealer and Joe. Your father saw the dealer hand Joe a package and an amount of cash change hands. It was an obvious drug deal. Your parents' fate was sealed from that moment. The dealer was working for the Trio and was scared of the repercussions if your dad said anything about the incident."

"Did Joe tell you who the police officer was?"

"He didn't know the name, but it was a woman — middle-aged, he said."

Rachel looked at Lee closely. The girl was deadly serious, not spinning her a yarn.

"My parents were killed in a car crash. How does that square with what you've just told me?" she asked.

"Joe said he and the dealer pursued them and forced their car off the road. They hit a tree at speed and the rest you know."

Rachel felt the tears well in her eyes. She couldn't listen to this. If Lee was telling the truth, then her parents had been murdered. She nudged Elwyn and got to her feet. "I'm sending Kenton in."

Out in the corridor, Rachel leaned against the wall. Kenton had left the room next door and came to join her. "You heard that, sir. I can't sit in there any longer."

"Go and make a drink, Rachel. I'll finish here and decide what do with the girl."

Rachel was shaking. A woman detective, high-ranking. How high? DCI? She made herself a mug of strong coffee and stared out of the window. Nell Hennessey had warned her off the case all those months ago, and today she was living in style in a house way above her pay grade. The thoughts circling inside her head made Rachel feel sick.

CHAPTER THIRTY

Rachel was upset and in no mood to hang around for the end of Lee's interview. She'd heard enough and needed to think. The problem of Jed and Blackmore was one thing, but now she had to consider whether Nell Hennessey was corrupt. Or had she got that terribly wrong? Was she so overwrought about the case and Jed's involvement that she couldn't think straight?

The journey home was straightforward enough except for road works on the junction by the Rising Sun pub in Hazel Grove. The sign said they'd continue for the next six weeks, so she'd have to factor the extra time into her journey. If she was honest with herself, the distance she had to travel every day was getting her down. When she only had the girls to think about and Alan living next door, it hadn't seemed too bad. Now, with little Len in the mix it was two daily journeys she could do without.

She arrived at the cottage to find the place empty — no Jed and no kids. There was a note on the kitchen table. Jed had taken both Mia and Len to her ex-husband Alan's in Bollington. Apparently, during the time it had taken her to drive home, the interview with Kenton had become urgent. Blackmore's PM results must be through. The fact that they needed Jed at the station didn't bode well. The only piece of evidence she had to cling to was Lee's insistence that whoever was after the Trio was female.

Rachel drove the few miles to Bollington to pick up the kids. Alan was helping Mia with her homework and his partner, Belinda, was playing with Len on the sitting room rug.

She beamed up at Rachel. "He's a gorgeous little lad, no trouble at all. I don't know how you can bear to leave him all day."

"It is hard, but I have to work." Rachel tried to smile. "And he might look the little angel now, but you should hear him at three in the morning. Thanks for having them at such short notice, Belinda. I don't know what Jed was thinking of. He should have insisted on waiting for me to come home."

"Urgent he said, and he wouldn't have troubled us otherwise. But Mia is Alan's child after all, and he does miss her."

Rachel was too tired for conversation. All she wanted was to grab the kids, go home and get Len to bed. Then, perhaps, she'd have time to work all this out. "Mia can come anytime, but she's a teenager and you know what that means — always closeted in her room on her mobile talking to this friend or that. I barely see her to talk to myself these days and we live in the same house, never mind spending time with Alan."

"Alan wants her to come away with us next month, down to Cornwall. We've rented a cottage for a couple of weeks. D'you think she'd like that?"

"Ask her. If she's happy to go, then I've no objection."

"Rachel." It was Alan, her ex-husband. "Good to see you, and the kids. Megan okay?"

Rachel nodded. "Belinda's just told me about Cornwall. I think it's a great idea, but I warn you she's at that moody teen stage. You may have your work cut out."

"I have asked her and she's okay with it. She wants to bring Chloe, so I'll have a word with her mum. If she agrees, then we're on."

"Two moody teens, you're a right glutton for punishment."

Rachel picked Len up from the rug, called to Mia and made her way to the front door. Belinda followed with the infant's bag.

"The stuff they need is something else," Rachel said, taking the bag from her and tossing it onto the back seat.

"Anytime you need us we're here. I know you work odd hours and I'm not averse to a spot of babysitting."

"Thanks, Belinda, I appreciate the offer. I did hope that me and Jed could work this out. However, his part of the deal is proving a little hard for him to keep. There's always some problem or other taking him off at all hours."

Belinda patted Rachel's hand. "Don't worry, these things have a habit of settling."

It took ten minutes to get home. The cottage was empty and strangely quiet. There was no text on her mobile from Jed, nor any messages on the house phone answer machine. Rachel got Len into his cot and then showered and put on a dressing gown. It was time to relax — if only her head would let her.

Kenton had heard Lee say the 'boss' attempting to oust the Trio was female. She was certain of it, even though she'd never met the woman, so that ruled out Jed. In that case, why keep him this long? If Lee was right, and Rachel could only pray that she was, who was this mysterious female? Well, she had some nerve, Rachel gave her that. The Trio's reputation was such that crossing them meant likely death.

A thought occurred to her. Rachel felt a shiver run through her body. Could it be Grace? Had she made a play for the role of gang leader? The thought was so outlandish that she dismissed it almost immediately as the product of a tired mind. Nonetheless, it would explain a number of things.

CHAPTER THIRTY-ONE

Day Five: Thursday

Jed got home at 5 a.m. Rachel heard the key in the front door and then the sound of the kettle downstairs. She got out of bed and went to join him.

"What kept you all this time?" she asked.

"Kenton and his questions."

He looked tired, pale and drawn, in no mood for an interrogation from her. "How's it been left?"

"Okay, I think. I reckon I've managed to convince him that I didn't kill Brendan Blackmore," he said flatly.

"Surely he doesn't think that."

"Oh, for a while there I think he did."

Rachel watched him slam the mug back on the worktop and take the whisky bottle from the cupboard instead.

"I've had a pig of a day and Kenton was the final straw. He made me feel like a cold-hearted killer."

Rachel rubbed his arm. "It's just his job. I take it Blackmore's death wasn't an accident then?"

"Hardly. He was left half-buried in the footings of one of the houses we're building. Unfortunately, whoever did it was a bit mean with the cement. His feet were sticking out. I hope to god he was dead before they put him there."

Rachel shuddered. "Poor man. Had he been left like that for long?"

"Long enough for the concrete to set," he said.

"What I don't understand is why your site."

"Me neither. Anyway, I'm too tired to think about it now. I need to sleep."

"Okay," Rachel said. "I'll take Len to nursery, and you can pick him up when you feel better."

Once Jed had gone upstairs Rachel made herself a coffee and went out into the garden. The sun was rising, it promised to be a pleasant day. She wished with all her heart that she could resolve this and prove conclusively that Jed was innocent. Despite his release from custody, she was still worried.

* * *

It had been one helluva night, but back at work Rachel did her level best to appear her usual self. She entered the main office and gestured for Elwyn to follow her. "Coffee in the canteen. I'd like a quiet chat."

"I wasn't privy to the interview with Jed, if that's what you're thinking," he said at once. "He had a sergeant from Baxter's team with him. You know what that means, Baxter will be crowing over this and chalking up all the extra brownie points he can get. He's been itching to get in on this case since the beginning. If it hadn't been for the Ardwick robberies, he would have been the SIO."

What DCI Baxter thought was of no interest to Rachel. "What about Lee? Did she have anything interesting to say, apart from the fact that it's a woman heading up the opposition to the Trio?" she asked.

"Not really, but Kenton went over it again with her after you left. She didn't deviate from her original statement, and I think Kenton was convinced."

"That's good," Rachel said. "Takes the pressure off Jed. What's Kenton done with Lee?"

"She's locked up downstairs. Don't forget she did kidnap the Agnew infant and Hutton's mother, and Edith hasn't turned up yet."

"Can't Lee help with that?" Rachel asked.

"She's no idea what this Ronzo did with her. Kenton intends to charge Lee, but he has given her the option of helping with the case. He wants her to flush out Ronzo. If she agrees, Kenton has promised to have a word with the CPS on her behalf."

Rachel frowned. "Lee back on the streets puts her in terrible danger. Anything goes wrong and it's her life we're risking."

"Well, Kenton thinks it's a risk worth taking. She'll be watched at all times."

Rachel considered this. Perhaps Kenton was right. Ronzo did need finding, and quick. He had vital information and could tell them who he was working for. "I want you to do something for me," she asked. "A bit of research and keep it quiet."

"Is it dodgy?"

"Might be." She raised her eyebrows. "But it could have an impact on the case. I want you to find out if there is any connection between Nell Hennessey and Grace Blackmore. Anything at all, no matter how small."

Elwyn gave a little whistle. "What's in your mind, Rachel? You haven't just plucked this out of thin air."

"It's like I told you — suddenly money is no object. Since Nell has retired, she's moved into a huge house and is having it customised for her mum. I want to know where the money has come from."

"Her pension pot?" Elwyn suggested.

"Wouldn't be enough. No, I think it's more complicated than that. Lee told us that my dad saw a female police officer talking to her friend Joe and a dealer on the forecourt of that garage. Not long after, they died in the crash. I think that officer was Nell."

"You think Nell Hennessey is working for the Trio?"

"Yes, I do and has been for some time now. It would explain a lot. Why she warned me off pursuing what Joe told me, and why none of the Trio are in prison."

"Will you tell Kenton?" Elwyn asked.

Rachel wasn't sure about that one. She pulled a face. "First I need solid proof. I can't go to Kenton on a hunch."

Elwyn nodded.

"There's something else. See what you can find out about a solicitor called Nigel Fortune, nickname 'Nidge'."

"Okay, but I'll have to save the research for later. It's Blackmore's PM this morning. Me and Kenton are down for that one."

"I'd like to know what Forensics find."

"I'll have a word with Jude. Anything comes up about Jed, I will tell you, Rachel."

CHAPTER THIRTY-TWO

Butterworth had just completed the PM on Brendan Blackmore, now covered in a white sheet. "He's taken a deal of cleaning up," he told Kenton and Elwyn, whisking the sheet away. "We've managed to get rid of the concrete but doing so has made the job of deciding which injuries were inflicted prior to death more difficult."

"D'you have a time of death?" Elwyn asked.

"Within the last twenty-four hours. We think he was kept somewhere, held prisoner and not given a lot to eat either. The stomach contents are meagre — just water and a little bread. We've taken blood samples to ascertain whether he was drugged." Butterworth took hold of one of the dead man's hands. "Look at this — the skin on his knuckles is broken and scabbed over. Maybe he fought when he was taken, but the fading bruises and the scabs tell us he was kept long enough for the healing process to start."

"Anything to suggest he was kept on that site?" Kenton asked.

"The concrete has made things difficult, but we did find traces of black paint under his fingernails. The site is still being searched and samples taken. Forensics find a building with this paint on the walls or woodwork, and you'll have your answer."

Kenton beckoned to Jude. "Make that a priority please. It's vital we know where Blackmore was held. When we do, we'll have a suspect."

"Concrete aside, his clothing might give us something too," Jude said. "There's blood on the shirt and jacket, his most likely, but you never know."

"While you're looking at DNA, check the database and look at Jed McAteer in particular," Kenton said.

"You think McAteer is responsible for this?" Jude asked.

"No, but it's important to rule him out given where the body was found." Kenton turned back to Butterworth. "How did he die?"

"A bullet to the temple." Butterworth pointed. "Went in here and exited here. We have retrieved it. He was put in the foundations and shot where he lay. In addition to the injuries to the knuckles, there's bruising on all four limbs and the torso."

"He was beaten?" Elwyn asked.

"Looks that way."

"Taken, beaten and kept locked up without food, then shot through the head. Why the concrete, I wonder? If it was to hide the body, they didn't do a good job of it," Elwyn said.

"The beating happened first and then he was taken to where he was killed."

"You sure he wasn't dumped there already dead?" Elwyn asked.

"No," Butterworth said. "We found concrete in his airway. Not much but enough to suggest that he inhaled a few times before being shot in the head."

"I don't get it," Kenton said. "There was plenty of opportunity to hide the body properly."

"Perhaps whoever killed Mr Blackmore wanted him found," Jude suggested.

"A bit gruesome, leaving him on display like that," Kenton said.

Jude shrugged. "A lesson to others perhaps, Superintendent?"

* * *

Rachel felt like a spare part. She wasn't allowed to be involved in the case, but given that Jed had been questioned and released, it was hard to take.

"Did you find anything on Joe Collins?" she asked Jonny.

"Not really. He was known, but apart from Lee he kept to himself mostly. I had a word with a woman in the soup kitchen and later that night with a bloke called Terry. Drew a blank I'm afraid."

Just as Rachel had suspected. Having once been beaten by the Trio, he wouldn't risk attracting their attention again.

"The woman in the soup kitchen recalled Lee too, said she'd been in with her sister and Joe. The three hung around together for a while," Jonny said.

"Anyone mention Ronzo?"

"No, ma'am."

Apart from a couple of uniforms the two of them were alone in the office.

"Where's Amy?" Rachel asked.

"Got the morning off."

"Any particular reason? Is she ill?"

Jonny looked sheepish. "I don't think so, but she'd cleared it with the super, so I didn't like to pry."

Rachel shook her head. A DC on her team playing fast and loose with work time when they had a heavy load on their hands. Kenton needed to get a grip.

"D'you have a hard copy of Lee's interview?" she asked.

"I can print one off," Jonny said. "But what if the super finds out?"

"Leave him to me — and I won't tell if you don't." She grinned.

Clutching a sheaf of papers, Rachel retired to her own office. She wanted to know what Lee had said, and particularly if she'd mentioned Jed or described anyone like him. Being out of the loop like this was doing her head in. The sooner Jed was ruled out, the better.

CHAPTER THIRTY-THREE

Elwyn returned to the station at lunchtime. He went straight to the canteen and rang Rachel on her mobile. "We should talk."

"You know something?"

"Not much, just the basics. Jude has more tests to do before we get anything positive."

The basics? What did that mean? Rachel left her office and went to join him.

"Kenton dropped me in the car park and went straight up to his office," Elwyn said. "We'll sit over there out of sight. It's not a good idea for him to see us talking like this. The man's not daft, he'll know we're discussing the case."

"What did you discover?"

"Blackmore was badly beaten and held somewhere. He wasn't fed much and a few days later was shot in the head. Jude is testing paint found under his fingernails and CSI are taking samples from the structures on Jed's site."

"Is there anything else that points to it being Jed that killed him?" she asked.

"Not so far."

"Why the concrete? What did Jude say about that?"

"He took his last breaths after he was dumped in the pit where the foundations were to be laid. He must have lain there badly injured while they poured concrete over him. But they didn't do a good job. His arms and legs were sticking out, and his forehead where they shot him. Jude reckons he was shot just before the concrete was poured, because he inhaled some. The concrete might have been an attempt to bugger up the forensics, or to make him talk, who knows?"

"So why leave him on view like that? Why not hide the body? It's a building site, it's not as if they were short of places."

"Disturbed perhaps?" Elwyn suggested.

Rachel shuddered. "If he'd been hidden properly no one would have been any the wiser. Paint aside, does Kenton think he was held on Jed's site?"

"He hasn't said, but Jude's people are all over it, taking samples from everywhere. Let's hope for Jed's sake she doesn't find anything."

"I want him ruling out, Elwyn," Rachel said firmly. "I want my job back. This sitting on the sidelines isn't doing me any good. I hope Kenton believes Lee's assertion that it's a woman leading the attempt to oust the Trio."

"We'll have to wait and see what Jude turns up. If there's nothing to incriminate Jed, I'm sure Kenton will see sense. I'm off back up to the office. I'll do that research for you."

"It's okay, Elwyn, I can do my own research now. After all, I'm not doing much else."

Elwyn finished eating and took his jacket from the chair back. "Okay, see you later."

As soon as she was alone Rachel rang Jude. "I won't compromise your position by asking awkward questions about Jed. This is about the Agnew infant. Did you find anything else on the seat or his clothing that might prove useful?"

"Other than the vomit, not yet. Everything is still being processed I'm afraid, Rachel. Kenton has primed me about your position, but that doesn't mean I can't drop the odd hint, particularly if I find anything to rule Jed out."

"It's looking pretty grim though. I'm not daft. From where I'm standing this has the old Jed written all over it.

Well, everything except the shooting. As far as I'm aware, he never actually killed anyone. But I will admit I've always been afraid to ask."

"The minute I've got something I'll tell you," Jude promised.

Blackmore's body being found on Jed's site was one complication too many. It was all she could think about. Rachel made her way back upstairs to her office. She'd been sitting at her computer for a good ten minutes when a movement in the main office caught her eye. It was Kenton. She went out to see what he wanted.

"Sergeant Pryce and I are off to speak to Grace," he told her. "Miss Lomax has asked to speak to you again. Keep her sweet, gain her trust, we're relying on her to help us."

Rachel nodded, although she wasn't sure that was a good idea. Lee was used to doing her own thing. For all they knew, rather than help them, the moment they let her loose on the streets, she'd try and run again.

* * *

"They're keeping me a bloody prisoner," Lee complained on seeing Rachel. "That wasn't part of the deal."

Rachel sat down opposite the girl and her solicitor. "You abducted a baby, Lee, and an elderly woman. We can't simply ignore that."

"I told you why I did those things," she said sulkily. "I was hurting. The Trio killed my sister and I wanted revenge."

"Was the kidnapping your idea?"

Lee shook her head. "That was down to Ronzo. I wanted to target Agnew and Hutton directly, do them harm, even kill them, but Ronzo wouldn't hear of it. He said targeting their families was a better idea."

Rachel couldn't see it. Surely, targeting members of the Trio directly would have cleared the path for the takeover. "Did he say why?"

"They are too useful, apparently. He said they knew things. I might want revenge, but he and his people want information. Taking the infant and the old woman was leverage."

"D'you know what information he wanted?"

"It was to do with the way their operation was organised. That's all he said. Ronzo was never that talkative."

"D'you know where Ronzo lives?" Rachel asked.

"No. I told the other bloke all this. I know nothing about him except that he calls himself Ronzo."

"I'm aware that Superintendent Kenton wants you to help us find him. He wants you to go back on the streets, so he'll come after you. How d'you feel about that?"

"It's risky but it might work." She looked Rachel in the eye. "I don't have a lot of choice, do I? Refuse to play the game and I go down for a long time."

"You'd be watched. The risk to yourself would be minimal."

Lee shook her head. "The risks are still there though. And what if he's not interested in me anymore? After all, what can I tell you?" She laughed. "Not a lot 'cause I don't know owt, and Ronzo's well aware of that. On the other hand he could be out there just waiting to pounce. On my own, I mightn't even make it to the train station without being picked up." She gave a shrug. "They have a copper on side, you know that. What's to say Ronzo doesn't know everything that's going on with me in here? You let me out and it might work, or it might not." She stared at Rachel for a few seconds. "If I was you, I'd stack the odds in your favour. Ensure Ronzo knows what's happening. That way he's sure to show his hand."

"How do I do that, Lee?"

"Make sure that bent copper has a word in the right ear."

CHAPTER THIRTY-FOUR

A word in the right ear. Lee was a clever girl. She wanted Rachel
to shorten the odds on trapping Ronzo, make sure the bent
copper, whoever that was, knew all about the plans and then
set a trap to catch Ronzo. But who was the bent copper? Nell?
She was no longer in the force and not privy to any of their
plans, but Lee didn't know that. Rachel had a better idea.
Never mind relying on someone they couldn't control, she
preferred the direct approach.

First, Rachel wanted to know if Nell was working for
the Trio. If so, she might have heard something, know who
wanted them out. Right or wrong it was worth asking her
because Rachel and the team needed all the edge they could
get. But first there was the research. Rachel had to satisfy
herself that Nell was indeed corrupt.

Back in the main office, she collared Jonny. "I want
you to find all the information you can on Grace Blackmore
and keep it quiet, especially from Amy. You find something,
bring it straight to me."

Rachel went to her office and began her research. As
expected, Nell's work record was excellent. A good clear-up
rate, a happy team and no hint of anything untoward.
Whatever her link with the Trio was it had nothing to do

with her professional life. Next, her private life. Rachel went through the birth and marriage records. Her parents were fairly average, hard working with ordinary jobs. Nell had never married so she hadn't changed her name. The story she'd told about her mother's sister, Diane, was true in so far as the woman had existed. She'd married a Geoff Winter, again no children, and had lived in Huddersfield. But the bit about the money was a lie, there was no record of probate. At the time of Diane's death she'd been living in social housing and had several county court judgements pending against her. It appeared Nell's sister paid very few of her bills. She owed everyone — utilities, rent and a number of credit card companies. The tale about the house in Oxford had been a blatant lie.

Further research provided the answer. After the death of Nell's aunt, Diane, Nell's mother had taken out a loan from 'Hewitt Finance,' the company owned by Grace Blackmore's grandfather, to pay off the lot.

Rachel went for a word with Jonny. "What happened to old man Hewitt's business after his death?"

"I was just looking at that, ma'am, as part of my research into Grace Blackmore. Grace was a partner in her grandad's firm. When the old man died, she inherited. I presume it got swallowed up in the Trio's many enterprises."

Rachel nodded but didn't comment. She didn't want to share her suspicions with Jonny just yet. But the information was interesting. It meant that Nell's mother was in hock to the Trio and had been for some time. Dee had long-standing dementia, she'd not realise the danger, but Nell would. Had she thrown in her lot with the gang in order to protect and provide for her mother? Time to find out.

"I'm off out. Kenton comes back you've no idea where I've gone," she told Jonny.

* * *

"What now, Rachel?" Nell said. "I hope it's something quick. I've got a lot on today."

Fair enough, so straight to the point. "You lied about Dee's sister, your aunt," Rachel said. "Diane Winter died up to her ears in debt, so there was no inheritance. There was no will and consequently no probate. Your mum took out a loan to pay it off. Not a good idea, given who lent her that money."

Nell looked stunned. "Utter rubbish. Where have you got this tale from? You're deluded. Who's told you these things?"

"The debts are a matter of public record, Nell. Push me and I can provide proof. I wouldn't come here and say these things without checking the facts first."

Nell looked deflated, as if Rachel had knocked the wind out of her. "You'd better come in I suppose. I'm not discussing this at the door." She led the way into the kitchen.

"I'm right, aren't I? Dee borrowed from Hewitt and when he died his granddaughter, Grace Blackmore, applied pressure. What did she want from you?"

Nell sank onto a chair. "I always knew this would happen, that one day someone would find me out. Once I retired, I hoped that perhaps I'd gotten away with it. But no, here you are, a self-righteous copper with a chip on her shoulder."

So that was how Nell saw her. Rachel gave a little smile. "Sorry, I'm simply doing my job. Your connection to Grace Blackmore has a bearing on our current case." Rachel sat down opposite her at the table. "Tell me what happened, how you got into this mess."

"It was simple enough. My Aunt Diane was dead and that evil bitch, Blackmore, persuaded Dee to take out a loan to pay off her sister's debts. I had no idea when or how she found Dee but then I was summoned to that huge house, and I knew. Grace Blackmore told me in no uncertain terms what my life would be like from then on. She'd write off Dee's debt and pay me to care for her if I did as she wanted." She looked at Rachel. "I should have reported the whole thing, but I didn't. The woman is evil. Grace knew my vulnerability — that I needed money for Dee's care — and she used it to her own advantage. It was so unfair. The debt wasn't

Dee's in the first place. She misguidedly thought she was helping clear her sister's name. If there had been any other way, I'd have taken it, but there wasn't. Grace made that clear enough. From that day forward I was on the payroll and had to toe the line."

So Nell was the bent copper Lee had spoken about. "Diane died five years ago. Is that how long you've been working for Grace Blackmore and the Trio?"

"Yes, although she hasn't asked for much. Lose the odd witness statement here and piece of evidence there. The cases involved weren't that serious and I told myself it wasn't really hurting anyone, nothing more than allowing one more dealer the freedom to ply his trade or gangster to continue his work."

"You knew my dad, didn't you? He was a barrister. He saw you with a known drug dealer the night he and my mum were murdered."

Nell's head shot up and she looked Rachel in the eye. "I had nothing to do with that. I didn't know what they were going to do. When I read about the accident in the papers I was horrified. I spoke to Grace, and she told me never to mention it again. To ensure my silence, she gave me an extra twenty thousand pounds that month."

"The money she paid you over the years, that's what you've used to pay for Dee's care?"

"Every penny. Now I've bought this house and will convert it to suit her needs. She's my mother. I have to do what I can to make her comfortable," Nell said.

"Brendan Blackmore has been found dead. D'you know anything about that?" Rachel said.

"All I know is that he and Grace had a huge row two weeks ago. She rang and told me she wanted him watched. She suspected that he was seeing another woman."

That came as a surprise to Rachel. It was an angle she hadn't considered, and it sparked something in her mind. What if that was the reason Jed was absent from home so much? If he wasn't involved in any aspect of the case, maybe he was out most nights because of another woman? Did he find a life of kids and domesticity too boring after what he'd done before? The idea hit Rachel like a bombshell, making her wonder why she hadn't considered it before. "What exactly did she expect you to do?"

"Watch him, follow him around. I told her I couldn't possibly do such a thing, that I'm not in the job anymore and have my mother to look after, but she insisted." She gave a humourless laugh. "When Grace tells you to do something, believe me, you do it. The consequences of crossing her are not for the squeamish. She said this would be the last time she'd call on me. After this, I would get a generous pay-out and be free." She heaved a sigh. "Given my circumstances, it was too good an offer to pass up."

"Did you find out who this other woman was?"

"Yes, her name is Caroline Jones. She's young, blonde, very pretty and works at a café in the Arndale. I saw Brendan meet her from work one evening — they were all over each other. I rang Grace the following day and told her."

"How did she take it?"

"How d'you think? Grace is a proud woman, the idea that Brendan could do such a thing to her hurt her badly."

"Did she threaten him at all?" Rachel asked.

"Not as far as I know."

"He was missing a good while, now he turns up dead. Could Grace have done that?" Rachel asked.

"I reckon she's capable of anything. That woman is as hard as nails and has little in the way of a conscience. Yes, I think even killing her own husband wouldn't be beyond her, particularly as he was cheating on her."

"Thanks, Nell. What you've told me is useful," Rachel said.

"What happens to me now?"

Rachel shook her head. She knew what she should do but she didn't have the stomach for it right now. "I don't know. Either me or a colleague will be in touch."

"There is something you should know," Nell said. "It might help you and your colleagues to make up your minds.

You see, I wasn't the only detective working out of the Manchester stations that was passing on useful information and doing the Trio's bidding. There is at least one other, and this person is working in your own station."

Rachel sat down again. This was a shock. All she needed. "Got a name?"

Nell gave her a sly smile. "Oh yes, but I'm saving that for a deal."

At least she was honest.

"All I'm saying is that the officer I'm talking about was working for the Trio but has now transferred his allegiance. He's working for those who are taking over from them. In other words, he's sold out to the highest bidder."

"You know that for a fact?" Rachel asked.

"Yes."

"You could help us, Nell, help us bring in an important member of this gang."

"Not without a deal. I've got Dee to think of. And a word of advice, don't make your plans for the girl common knowledge. Better keep the details to the people you can really trust."

CHAPTER THIRTY-FIVE

Nell Hennessey had given Rachel a lot to think about. Another bent copper in the camp. What she didn't know was whether he'd got his act together fast enough to interfere with the case.

Another teaser Nell had given her was the possibility that Blackmore's death had nothing to do with the Trio and wasn't linked to what had happened to Agnew and Hutton either. Instead, it was down to a spat between Brendan and Grace. That one needed investigating before it could be ruled in or out.

Rachel left Nell and made her way to the Arndale Centre in central Manchester. She knew the café and could only hope that Caroline Jones was working today. Even if this didn't prove Jed's innocence entirely, it gave Kenton another line of enquiry.

The Arcade Café was on the ground floor, a fast-food place with half a dozen tables. It was busy, with the four staff working their socks off. Only one of the young women was blonde.

"Caroline?" Rachel asked flashing her warrant card. "DCI King, East Manchester CID. Can I have a word?"

The girl looked warily towards the kitchen door. "Have you seen how busy we are? The manager will go mental."

"It can't be helped. I'm investigating a murder."

That shook her. Straight away Caroline put down the tray she'd been carrying and followed Rachel to an empty table.

"Brendan Blackmore, you knew him."

The girl nodded. "Yes, he's a good bloke."

That was a matter of opinion. "I'm afraid I've got some bad news. Mr Blackmore is dead, murdered. When did you see him last?"

"A week ago. He rang me, wanted to meet but he didn't turn up and there's been no calls, texts or anything. I presumed he'd changed his mind and wanted to finish it." She took out a hankie and dabbed her eyes. "This is dreadful. Murdered you said? I don't understand, who'd want to kill him? He was such a nice bloke."

"How long had you been seeing him?"

"Six months or so. We met just out there." She pointed to some seats outside. "He was in a rush and slipped on a drink someone had spilled. I sat him down and got him a coffee. I didn't think anything more of it, but the next day he turned up with a huge bunch of flowers. He asked me out and we went from there."

"Did you know he was married?" Rachel asked.

She shook her head and began to cry in earnest. "I had no idea. He told me his wife was dead."

Grace was far from that. Rachel handed Caroline a card. "Either me or one of my colleagues may want another word."

* * *

Rachel returned to the station. Despite being told to leave the case alone, this was important information and Kenton needed to know. A quick chat with Elwyn first, to see if Grace had told them anything important.

"I'd say she took it well," he said. "Given how long they'd been together, she wasn't the emotional mess I expected. It'll probably hit her later."

"Not if she'd killed him out of jealousy it won't," Rachel said. "We'll catch up when I've spoken to Kenton."

Rachel walked along the corridor to the super's office, tapped on the door and went in. "I need a word."

"Important, is it?"

"Could be, could even be vital." Rachel sat down opposite Kenton and told him about her initial suspicions and the meeting with Nell Hennessey. She couldn't tell from his expression whether he was surprised at this or not. "We can't rule out that Brendan's death could be down to his infidelity — Grace getting even," she concluded. "If it is, that young woman could be in danger."

After a seemingly unending silence, Kenton finally said, "I'll make sure the vicinity of that café is patrolled regularly, and I'll alert the security staff at the Arndale."

"Thanks, sir, that makes me feel better."

"But I told you not to get involved. I turn my back for half a day, and you jump in feet first."

"I had no idea Nell had anything to do with this, sir," she said. "I wanted to ask her about something else — the death of my parents."

"That young man, Joe Collins. Nell warned you off him months ago. We now know he once worked for the Trio, so you must have guessed she knew something," Kenton said.

Rachel pulled a face. "Instinct, sir. I suspected she knew things that could help us."

Kenton shook his head. "We spoke to Grace for over an hour and she made no mention of this Caroline Jones or any other woman Brendan could have been seeing. I did ask her more than once."

"That could be because she'd dealt with it herself, sir," Rachel suggested. "That this entire 'my husband's missing' thing is a cover-up for what really happened."

"We still have to consider what happened to the Agnew child and Hutton's mother. That can't have anything to do with a jealous wife."

"Who knows? Perhaps Grace wanted to make it look like all of them were being targeted. You know, divert attention from a failing marriage."

"I'm not sure, Rachel. For a start, Grace is more likely to have had Caroline Jones killed than Brendan."

"Depends how much she knew. Whether she tackled Brendan about the affair and what he told her."

Kenton nodded. "The Blackmore marriage aside, we've still got the problem of Ronzo and the murder of two young people. We'll release the girl, Lee, tomorrow lunchtime. We'll make sure she's watched and her calls monitored. If Ronzo makes any attempt to contact her, we'll trace him."

"We can't guarantee that Ronzo is even interested in the girl anymore," Rachel said.

"What choice do we have? She's our only lead. Without her, catching up with him could take weeks. Think of the mayhem he could be responsible for in the meantime," Kenton said. "We let her go and hope he's watching and makes a play to get her back onside."

"We could stack the odds in our favour," Rachel said. "We release Lee but before she leaves the station, we get her to ring Ronzo and ask him to pick her up."

Kenton considered this. "It wouldn't be so risky with adequate protection."

"She could tell him she wants help to continue her vendetta against the Trio. Ronzo would accept that. It's what made her so useful to him in the first place."

"I'm still not sure."

"We release Lee with nothing in place, sir, and what's to say Ronzo won't catch up with her anyway? We can't watch her forever. It could be her body we find in an alley next. It's worth a try and I'm sure she'll go for it, danger and all."

Kenton took a few moments to think about it. "Okay, go ahead and organise it."

"Nell told me something else, it's more important than Brendan's infidelity. You're not going to like this, sir, but she said we have a copper in this station who was working for the Trio but has now shifted his allegiance to Ronzo and his crew."

Kenton did not look happy. "Did she give you a name?"

"No, she wants to use what she knows to cut a deal."

Kenton shook his head. "An officer here? Someone on our own team?"

"So Nell said. If it's true, we need to be very careful what information we share."

"Okay, we keep our plans for the young woman to you, me and DS Pryce. You and Pryce will take her to whatever location she and this Ronzo agree on, release her and be on hand to watch out for him."

"That's a little risky, sir. Ronzo turns up mob-handed, me and Elwyn will be no match for them."

"Once you've decided on the location, we'll use a team of plain-clothed officers from my old station. They'll be on hand to ensure no harm comes to any of you."

With the extra bodies at the scene it should be safe enough. Now for the big one. Rachel cleared her throat. "Have you found any evidence against Jed?"

He smiled. "Loyal to the end. But to be fair, there is nothing. No forensics that I'm aware of and no motive either. Leaving Brendan like that on Jed's site could have been a case of sour grapes for something in the past. Plus, Lee was certain that the group working to oust the Trio was being led by a woman, and I believe her."

That was one huge relief. "Am I back on the case, then?"

"Given we have a new set of leads, I don't see why not."

* * *

Rachel returned to the main office and gave the team the good news. "Elwyn, a word in my office, please."

He followed her in. "Not trouble I hope? Kenton's not put conditions on you being back on?"

"No, all's well on that score. We're releasing Lee tomorrow but not a word. You, me and Kenton are the only three to know. We've got a bent copper in the station."

"Are you sure?"

"Yes. He was working for the Trio but has now swapped sides for Ronzo's lot. We are going to use Lee as bait to trap Ronzo, but we don't want it getting back to those in charge of him. In the morning we take her to a location of our choosing and she'll ring him, ask him to pick her up. Us two and some of Kenton's old team will be waiting."

Elwyn didn't look too happy. "We'll be taking a risk with Lee's life. Will she go with it?"

"If she wants to be free, then yes. But there is something else, and this is more personal. I want you to do something for me and keep this quiet as well."

"Is it connected to the case?"

"Could be, I just can't make up my mind. But whatever happens, I won't drop you in it. Any flak, I'll take the lot."

Elwyn smiled. "Come on then, what d'you want me to do?"

"Follow Jed for me. He's been going out most nights, sometimes not coming back while morning and I need to know what he's up to."

"D'you suspect another woman?" Elwyn asked.

Rachel didn't want to say. Elwyn had been privy to the ups and downs of her romance with Jed for a long time now, and she didn't want to admit defeat. "I've no idea, but at least knowing where he goes and who he sees would ease my mind, even if it does involve another woman. Say if you don't want to do this. If Jed was to spot you, he'd guess I'd put you up to it and I can't vouch for his actions. He's got a temper and I wouldn't want you on the wrong side of it."

"Don't worry Rachel, I'll be discreet."

CHAPTER THIRTY-SIX

Rachel had to believe that Jed had nothing to do with the case, her sanity depended on it. But it didn't stop the niggle. If he wasn't seeing someone else, where was he going? All this disappearing for hours at night on the back of a phone call made her suspicious. Instinct told her there was more to it than a dodgy piece of land.

Rachel handed Jed a glass of wine and sat beside him on the sofa.

"I had a call from Kenton." Jed smiled. "Seems I'm no longer a person of interest."

"Good news. About time he realised what was staring him in the face."

"You had your doubts too, didn't you? I saw the looks, the questions flying around in your head."

She grinned. "Just for a moment. But I know you're not a gangster anymore."

"Too bloody true. I don't have the stomach for it. So, who's in the frame now?" he asked.

Rachel sat back and sipped on her wine. "We're not really sure. We are looking for someone in particular. Once he's been interviewed, we'll know more. Finding him will be tricky though, we only know his first name."

"Can I help?"

"I doubt it, unless the name Ronzo means anything to you."

Jed shook his head, his expression giving nothing away.

"Pity. He's behind the kidnappings and who knows what else." Rachel knew she was taking a risk telling Jed this but she wanted to see his reaction.

"I thought that was down to some girl," he said.

"Yes, but Ronzo was pulling the strings," Rachel said.

"Can't she help you?" Jed asked.

"All she knows is his name. Anyway, she's got bail and will be released in the morning. We're using her as bait. Hopefully Ronzo will be watching, and he'll try to pick her up."

"A long shot I'd have thought. How d'you know this Ronzo will be in the right place at the right time?"

"If he's interested, he will be and that's all I'm saying," she said.

"And the girl's agreed to this?"

Jed had been asking a lot of questions. He wasn't usually so interested in her cases. That reinforced Rachel's suspicions that he was fishing. "Yes, it's part of a deal. I just hope she stays out of trouble and keeps to her bail conditions." Rachel poured them more wine. "This is perfect. Len in bed, Mia at Chloe's and we've nothing better to do than relax. Exactly how I like it."

Jed put his full glass down on the coffee table. "Sorry to disappoint, love, but I've got to go out."

Here they were, the words Rachel had been half expecting. "Not that bloody site again?"

"No, that's still taped up and inaccessible to all but you lot. Heaven knows when work will resume. It's a meeting with a builder friend of mine. We're discussing plans for the next project. Might as well get on with something new while the houses are on hold. You've seen the state of the finances, I can't afford not to."

"Can't you do meetings in the daytime, or even bring people here? You could invite this builder round. I wouldn't mind."

"It'd bore you to death. No, better we do it at my office in town. I shouldn't be long, back before eleven."

The moment Jed left the house, Rachel rang Elwyn. "Where are you?"

"Parked by the village green in Poynton."

Now she felt guilty. Poor Elwyn, hanging around in his car waiting for her call. "Sorry you've had to wait with no guarantee that Jed would leave the house tonight, but he has, just as I anticipated."

"Just as well I'm here then."

"He said he was going to the office in town to meet with a builder."

"Leave it to me, Rachel," he said. "But I'll tell you this much. He's driven out of your lane and taken the Macclesfield turn."

Rachel felt her stomach churn. That was in the wrong direction. Why lie? Why say he was off to the office in Manchester if he wasn't? "Thanks for this, Elwyn. Keep a close eye, I'll wait for your call."

* * *

Elwyn followed Jed's black sports car to a pub on the outskirts of Macclesfield. Elwyn pulled up a little way back and watched him park up and go inside.

Tricky. Jed knew him so there was no way he'd get away with following him inside. There was nothing to do but sit it out. He didn't have to wait long. Within minutes, Jed appeared in the pub doorway with a man Elwyn didn't recognise. Mobile at the ready, he took a few photos. With luck, in this light and at this distance the quality wouldn't be too bad.

The two men drove off in separate cars. Elwyn noted that Jed headed back towards Poynton. He rang Rachel.

"He met a man in a pub this side of Macclesfield. Whatever the meeting was about it took all of ten minutes."

"Thanks, Elwyn, Jed's just phoned to say he's on his way home. His builder friend was called away, so that's why the meeting was cut short."

"Right then, I'll get off home. See you in the morning."

"Night, Elwyn, drive carefully."

CHAPTER THIRTY-SEVEN

Day Six: Friday

Rachel and Kenton were in his office, Kenton giving her his final instructions. "We've got several plain-clothed officers from my old station on this. They are already positioned at your suggested location on Pollard Street. You and Pryce will take the young woman there and make sure she makes that phone call. Once she sets off on her own, watch her like a hawk. We can't afford to lose her. One of you has eyes on her at all times and you maintain radio contact. Do I make myself clear?"

Rachel nodded. "When this is done, we'll have to get Lee to a safe house. Remember we have a bent copper in the station. Even with Ronzo in custody she still won't be safe. Word will get out and others will be looking for her."

"Very well. I'll deal with that while you apprehend Ronzo," he said.

Rachel left Kenton's office and went to see Lee, who was waiting with Elwyn in an interview room.

"Has Elwyn told you the plan? We've got plenty of people in the area, so you'll be safe, no need to be nervous," Rachel said.

"Pollard Street?" Lee asked.

"Yes, as you know it's a straight wide road with enough places for our people to watch and be ready to act."

Lee looked at the map Elwyn had spread out on the table.

"There won't be time for anything to go wrong," Rachel told her. "You call, Ronzo comes to get you and we pounce. It'll be quick and clean."

"You make it sound simple, but it's not," Lee said. "The people after me are killers. If by some fluke I do get picked up by Ronzo or his men, it's likely I won't live to see the end of the day."

"We'll have your back. You have to trust us, Lee."

Lee kept her eyes fixed on the map.

"Shortly, Elwyn will take you to the car. I'll get your things. We've made sure your mobile is charged up."

Rachel returned to the main office, where Jonny and Amy were deep in conversation.

"She's getting out then?" Amy asked.

"Possibly," Rachel said. She wasn't giving anything away.

"Mistake. Bail her or whatever and that's the last you'll see. That girl will disappear in seconds. You're forgetting the streets are her home, she knows people who'll hide her."

Since her romance with Kenton the young woman had become considerably more opinionated than before. Her attitude was an irritation Rachel could do without

"Want to share what's troubling you, Amy?"

"She knows others living on the streets like her. What's to say she hasn't got her way out planned and intends to make fools of us all."

"Do I have to remind you that Lee has been locked up. She's had no way to contact anyone. When she leaves here, she'll get her mobile back, but I doubt she'll have time to organise anything."

"I'm just saying. The girl is desperate and has nothing to lose."

* * *

The closer they got to the drop-off point, the more nervous Lee became. She fiddled with her phone, tapped her feet and kept glancing up and down the road.

"You'll be watching me all the time? You promise he won't get near?" she asked.

"Rest assured, Lee, we have your back. You see Ronzo's car or anyone else approaches you, you give the signal. One of the team will see it and act."

"He's a shifty bugger. You'll have to be quick."

"Don't worry about that." Rachel smiled. "We can be shifty ourselves when a situation demands it."

Elwyn pulled up halfway down Pollard Street. "Make the call. Ask him how long and we'll let you out in good time. It's a straight walk down there towards the station."

Rachel handed Lee her rucksack. The girl's hands were shaking as she punched in the number and put her phone on loudspeaker. It took only seconds for her to get a result.

"Good to hear your voice," Ronzo said.

"I need to see you," Lee said. "I can't finish the job on my own."

The young man laughed. "It doesn't work like that, Lee. You ran out on me. That has consequences."

"Okay, I ran, I admit it. But I was scared. I'm back now. All I want is the other members of the Trio dead, and this whole thing over and done with."

"I'll pick you up. Where are you?"

"Pollard Street."

She finished the call and looked at the two detectives. "That's it. Done. I should go."

Rachel patted her shoulder. "Take it slow and keep an eye out for his car. Elwyn will follow behind at a distance. I'll alert the others."

Lee got out of the car. Shrugging her shoulders, she fixed her rucksack securely on her back, then bent down and tightened the laces on her trainers. She took a deep breath and made her way down the street, turning to stare at every car that passed.

Rachel watched her go. This had to work. It was their one chance of arresting an important member of the gang behind the Trio takeover, the kidnaps and the murder of Brendan Blackmore.

Elwyn got out next and followed on foot at a safe distance from Lee. Rachel waited until they were several metres away before slowly driving closer. A quick glance to the right and she saw another of their cars with two plain clothes officers in it. Everything was in place.

It was Rachel who saw the silver car first, in her rear mirror. The driver was travelling at speed and drew up by Lee with a shriek of brakes.

Rachel closed the gap in seconds, slewed to a halt in front of the vehicle and radioed the others in the vicinity.

"Get in!" yelled the driver of the silver car.

Lee took no notice. She backed off, hitched up her rucksack and ran like the very devil himself was after her. Within seconds she'd reached the junction with Chapeltown Street and had disappeared from sight. It all happened so fast it took Rachel unawares, and all she could do was blink. For once, Amy had had been right. "We should have anticipated that," she growled.

"I don't think I've seen anyone move so fast," Elwyn added.

"What's this? What's happening?" Ronzo screamed at them. "Jesus! The bitch has stitched me up."

"She's dropped you in it, big-style," Rachel said with a grin. Elwyn dragged him out of the car and snapped on the handcuffs. "You're under arrest."

CHAPTER THIRTY-EIGHT

Elwyn and one of the plain-clothed officers borrowed from Kenton's old station took Ronzo back to the station, while Rachel sat in her car and tried to ring Lee. No response. What was the girl playing at? Rachel had no choice but to leave a message: 'Give yourself up, Lee, and we'll help you. You'll be safer with us than on the streets. We have Ronzo, he might no longer be a threat but we know he isn't working on his own.'

Moments later Lee called back. Hopefully the girl had seen sense, but her first words were, "I'm not going back inside. You want me, you'll have to find me and drag me back. I've helped you get Ronzo — that was the deal, so I'm free now, debt paid."

"It doesn't work like that, Lee. We just can't forget what you've done. You kidnapped the Agnew baby and Mrs Hutton, who's still missing."

"I helped with the kidnappings, that's all. I didn't harm either of them."

"That will be taken into consideration. You'll get an opportunity to put your side of things," Rachel said.

"No. I'm gone. I've done my bit. I'm leaving you lot and this miserable city for good."

The line went dead. Rachel tried ringing her back, but the phone was either switched off or Lee had ditched it.

* * *

Back at the station, Rachel went to see Kenton. She needed to bring him up to speed with the arrest and tell him about Lee. Not something she was looking forward to. Ronzo might be under lock and key, but Lee had escaped them and was still at large.

"It mostly went as planned," she began. "Ronzo didn't have time to do much else other than give up. We arrested him and he's in the cells awaiting interview."

"Mostly? Was there a problem?"

"Lee got away from us." This was bad. Kenton would blame her. Rachel held her breath.

"How could you let that happen? You were close by, DS Pryce was following her on foot, so what went wrong?"

"The girl is fast on her feet. Once we'd got Ronzo, she saw her chance and took it. She flew down Pollard Street like the wind. Lee knows the back streets and alleyways of this city like the back of her hand. She could be anywhere by now. And I believe she's ditched her mobile."

Kenton muttered something and banged down the file he'd been reading on his desk — hard. "So, what do we tell the CPS? I was just going over what we have on the girl."

"She might turn up, sir," Rachel offered. It sounded weak, even to her.

"That's very unlikely as well you know, but we'll issue an alert and description. Perhaps put something out on the media." He glared at Rachel. "I'm not happy with this outcome. That girl is guilty of kidnap and who knows what else. This plan of yours was supposed to work. You should have anticipated this."

"Look, I take full responsibility but there wasn't much we could do. I think Lee intended all along to escape like this."

Kenton still didn't look happy but he gave up for the time being. "Ronzo is in the cells?"

"Yes."

"Once he's processed, we'll interview him together."

"You want in too?" Rachel was surprised. Kenton didn't usually take such a close interest in the people they arrested.

"Yes. I want to know where the Hutton woman is and why Blackmore was killed."

"About half an hour. That suit you?"

Kenton nodded.

* * *

Rachel returned to her office and phoned Jude. Elwyn had had Ronzo's silver car taken to Forensics, so by now her people should be all over it.

"We know what to look for," Jude assured her. "Vomit for starters. The Agnew infant was sick during the kidnap, remember. Once you have the clothing the young man was picked up in, we'll look at that too."

"I'd appreciate anything you find as soon as. Kenton and I will be interviewing him, and I need it to go well. Lee made a run for it on Pollard Street and we lost her, so I can't afford any more mistakes or delays."

"I understand, Rachel. But you shouldn't beat yourself up. Lee was a decoy. It was a good plan but a girl like her — wild, lives on the streets — there's no pinning her down."

"That's not how Kenton sees it. Hopefully, we'll get an address out of Ronzo when we interview him. That will need to be searched too. Sorry, Jude, we have to rush this one, Edith Hutton is still missing."

"Don't worry about this end. Get an address and we'll do a thorough search. If he's your man, we'll get the evidence you need."

Rachel trusted Jude to do her part, but would Ronzo give them anything? Would he even reveal where he'd been living, never mind who he was working for? Time to find out.

CHAPTER THIRTY-NINE

Ronzo turned out to be more cooperative than Rachel had expected. He gave the officer processing him his full name and current address, as well as the clothes he was wearing when arrested, a DNA sample and his fingerprints, all without argument.

He sat in the interview room in a police-issue tracksuit, a self-satisfied look on his face. He was in his mid-twenties and of medium build — definitely not the man on the health centre CCTV.

"This is my solicitor, Nigel Fortune," he said. "We've had a little chat and I'm giving you nowt without his say-so."

Rachel sat down facing him with his file in front of her. "No problem, Mr Wade, we've plenty of time."

"Call me Ronzo, everyone does. You got that bitch Lee here too then?"

Rachel shook her head noncommittally. "Sorry, but I'm not at liberty to say."

"You have, haven't you? You've got her locked up. Serves her right for double-crossing me."

Kenton entered the room and sat down next to Rachel. "I'm Superintendent Kenton, and this is DCI King," he said.

"Ronald Wade you know, and I'm his solicitor, Nigel Fortune."

This came as a surprise to Rachel. Fortune was the old friend Jed had spoken of. Why him? Should she read anything into him being here? Probably not, he was a solicitor. But Jed had said he was expensive, so what was he doing representing this no mark? "Mr Fortune, I take it you're not the duty solicitor?"

"No, Mr Wade hired me."

So how did the villain know Fortune? Jed had hinted that the lawyer had a murky past — was he still dabbling? If so, did Jed realise this? The questions raged round in her head.

"Ronald Wade, street name, 'Ronzo,'" Kenton began. "You are charged with a number of offences, not the least of these being suspected murder."

Ronzo stared open mouthed at Kenton. "Not me, mate, you got the wrong bloke. I might frighten folk a little, but I don't kill them."

"Joe Collins, tell me about him," Kenton said.

"That loser," Ronzo scoffed. "Lived on the streets with that bitch you've got locked up. Why would I bother with him?"

Rachel was listening to this with half an ear, her attention on Fortune. She was trying to work out what his game was, where he fitted into it all. He must know she was Jed's partner.

"Who are you working for?" Rachel asked.

Ronzo gave her a stupid grin, stuck his hands in his pockets and shook his head.

"Speak to us and it could work in your favour," she said.

Ronzo laughed. "I doubt that. Tell you who the boss is, even if I knew, and I'll be dead before the end of the day."

"So there is a boss. Male or female, Ronzo? You see I heard you were working for a woman." Rachel remembered what Lee had told them.

Ronzo looked at Fortune who shook his head. "No comment."

Rachel took that to mean Lee had been right.

"Tell us about the kidnaps then. Why was it necessary to take the infant and the Hutton woman?" she said.

Ronzo looked round at the others in the room. "I say stuff, admit what I did and you'll throw the book at me. I'm not stupid."

"Tell us about the people who gave the orders and we might talk about a deal," Rachel said. "Talking to us could work in your favour Ronzo."

"The money was good, too good to pass up on." He shrugged. "I'm not whiter than white, I admit it, but I don't kill people or do them much harm. Taking the kid and the old woman didn't hurt anyone."

"That's your opinion. Didn't you think about the grief you gave the infant's parents?" Rachel asked. "And what about the elderly woman, Hutton's mother? What happened to her?"

"Keep your wig on," he smirked cheekily. "The old biddy's fine, she's come to no harm."

Kenton was running out of patience. "They'll be no deals until we get her back. Who paid you?"

"Dunno. Dosh were left on my car seat."

They were getting nowhere.

"Okay, you don't want to say who hired you, but how did they make contact?" Rachel asked.

"Got a call on my mobile. Date, place and what to do. It was dead simple. Easy money."

"We've got your mobile, Ronzo," Rachel said. "Believe me, we'll check every call you made and received, same with the texts and any emails or websites you might have visited."

His eyes narrowed. The mention of his mobile had him rattled, Rachel could see it on his face.

"Did you know that the people who hired you were working against the Trio?" she asked.

He gave her a sly smile. "I found that out pretty quick. Word on the street has it that the Trio are finished."

"Are you sure of that? The Trio have a fierce reputation and they are brutal when it comes to reprisals," she said.

Ronzo shook his head. "I told you, the Trio are done. A new lot run Manchester now."

"Got any names?"

He gave Rachel a grin. "No idea. All I know is that they're good and well organised."

"Not that well organised, otherwise why kidnap an infant and an elderly lady? What use can they be to a bunch of gangsters?"

Ronzo took a minute. Rachel half expected him to cry ignorance, but he surprised her. "The new lot want information about how the Trio do things." He leaned towards her and whispered, "Where to buy the drugs from, who the Trio's contacts in other countries are. Then, once the drugs get here, who helps out at the ports. How the street gangs are organised. Basically, they want names and details that'll make the takeover easier. The family members we took were to be used to persuade certain Trio members to play ball."

"And Brendan Blackmore? What went wrong there?" Kenton asked.

"No idea. That was nowt to do with me. Brendan wasn't part of the deal, just the baby and the old woman."

"Where is Hutton's mother?" Kenton asked again. "Things will go a lot smoother for you once she is safe."

"All in good time," Ronzo winked. "I haven't got my deal yet."

"You said *certain* Trio members," Rachel said. "What d'you mean by that? Didn't you need information from all three of them?"

Ronzo's face broke into a grin. "Sharp one, aren't you? But you're right, the new regime only needed Hutton and Agnew to talk about their part in the operation."

"And did they?" she asked.

"Squealed like pigs, the both of them."

"Why not press Grace? You were holding her husband," Kenton asked.

"Not me, I've never met him. Anyway, Grace wasn't the problem."

Rachel saw Fortune nudge him. Had Ronzo said too much in implicating Grace? From the worried look on the solicitor's face and his reaction this wasn't where he wanted the interview to go.

"We are organising a warrant to search your address. We need to find the Hutton woman. We'll take a break while we wait for it and resume the interview later."

Rachel was surprised when Kenton changed the topic. Did he not consider Grace's involvement in this important, or was he simply concerned with more pressing matters?

"Search away, I've nothing to hide," Ronzo said.

Rachel thought him far too confident. There had to be evidence of what he'd done, and his home was favourite, plus the Trio must want him dead. Why in that case wasn't he afraid?

CHAPTER FORTY

Rachel and Kenton left the interview room and returned to the main office.

"The search warrant is being sorted, ma'am," Jonny told them. "The address we have for him is in Ancoats just minutes away." Rachel nodded back.

"Why didn't any of what we threw his way bother him? It should have done," she said to Kenton. "Ronzo kidnapped James Agnew and Edith Hutton and we believe that he killed Joe Collins. We have his car and there has to be further evidence somewhere — the clothes he was wearing for example — and of course where he lives."

"He said he'd never met Brendan either. What d'you think?" Kenton asked.

"I think he's lying, and I bet that brief of his put him up to it. Did you see Ronzo's reaction to Grace's name? I know it's a long shot but is it possible that she's the woman boss Lee heard mentioned?"

"That crossed my mind too," Kenton said. "If it is Grace we're up against, we've got some fight on our hands. You go and do the search with DS Pryce."

"What about Grace?" Rachel asked.

"Before we resume the interview, I'll have another word with her."

"Want me to get someone else to go with Elwyn and come with you?"

"No. I'll take DC Farrell."

Kenton left them to it. Rachel shook her head at Elwyn. "He's up to something."

Elwyn waved the warrant at her. "Let's get this done with. We can puzzle over Kenton's behaviour later."

Rachel grabbed her jacket and joined him. "Ronzo's brief is an old friend of Jed's," she told him. "And he could be dodgy. Jed reckons he's reformed like him but given who he's representing, I don't see it. I got the impression the pair of them were orchestrating the interview according to some sort of plan."

They were now at Elwyn's car. "I saw him earlier talking to the desk sergeant," Elwyn said. "I'll drive, but there's something I want to show you first." They sat in the car while Elwyn found the photo he had taken on his mobile while he was following Jed. "It's him," he said, passing it to her. "It was Fortune Jed met up with in that pub, not a builder."

Elwyn was right. The image wasn't too clear, but the man with Jed was definitely Fortune. So, why had Jed lied? Why not simply tell her he'd gone for a word with his old friend?

* * *

Rachel stared around Ronzo's apartment in amazement. The place was huge, opulent, not at all what she was expecting. She looked out of the floor-to-ceiling window at the view over the city. "He's a thug, a small-time dealer. What's he doing with a place like this? For starters it must cost a packet, and look how tidy it is. There's not even a cushion out of place."

Elwyn wasn't taking much notice. He was busy going through the kitchen drawers and cupboards. He called back to her. "There's nothing, Rachel, not even any food in the fridge."

Rachel walked down the corridor to the bedroom. Like the rest of the place it was immaculate. She opened the wardrobes, which were also empty. "He's lied to us, Elwyn. Ronzo doesn't live here at all. I don't know why, he must realise that we'd see that the minute we walked into the place." She took her mobile and rang Amy. "I want to know who owns the apartment, the one Ronzo said was his. It's urgent, so get on it straight away."

She went into the kitchen to find Elwyn. "You can stop searching. We're not going to find anything. He's tried to fool us, to pass it off as his home but from the look of it this place hasn't been lived in for some time. Several of the apartments in this block are for sale. This one looks like the show apartment to me."

"We took the keys from the belongings that were found on him when he was arrested."

"It's a set-up. There's nothing incriminating here, certainly nothing that will point to Ronzo being guilty of anything but more important, there's nothing to tell us where Edith is." Rachel was angry. Ronzo wasn't stupid so what was he playing at?

Rachel's mobile rang, it was Amy.

"The apartment, ma'am. It's a rental. It's currently empty, and the last tenant left six months ago."

"Do we have a name?"

"Yes, a businessman from Surrey but that's not the interesting bit. That apartment and several others in the block is listed as belonging to Grace Blackmore."

"Thanks, Amy. Has Superintendent Kenton left yet?"

"About ten minutes ago."

Rachel finished the call, rang Kenton and brought him up to speed.

"We've got plenty on Ronzo, Rachel."

"We still don't know where Hutton's mother is."

"In that case, come back to the station and speak to him again. Get a search warrant for the Blackmores' house too. I'm going there now to bring Grace into the station. We'll see if a change of environment makes her more talkative. Have a couple of uniforms follow me in a car."

CHAPTER FORTY-ONE

"Impressive place my apartment, isn't it?" Ronzo grinned at the detectives.

"Very nice," Rachel said. "Shame it's not yours. You lied to us. Why do that?"

Ronzo shrugged. "I was paid to."

"Who by?"

"No idea. Same format — phone call, money and keys left in my car."

"You're lying, Ronzo. I think you know very well who owns that apartment."

He looked at Fortune. "Why won't she believe a word I say? I've had enough of this. I want to leave now."

"I'm afraid we're a long way from that happening. You need to start being honest with us, Ronzo, then we'll decide whether you can go or not. For starters, I want your real address and the truth about who you're working for."

"I'm up for a deal, if that's what you want."

Fortune cleared his throat, whispered in Ronzo's ear and said to Rachel, "I'd like a word in private with my client."

"Certainly," Rachel said. "I'll give you fifteen minutes."

Rachel and Elwyn went back to the office to be met by Jude.

"Good news. We found vomit in Wade's car, and it was the Agnew infant's. We also found a small clutch bag containing some of Edith Hutton's belongings, notably a mobile phone with her son's number on it."

"Surely Ronzo, or Wade as you know him, would have spotted the bag," Rachel said.

"Not necessarily. Edith Hutton had pushed it down the back of the seat."

This was good news. They now had tangible evidence needed to charge Ronzo with the kidnaps. James Agnew might have turned up, but they still had no idea what had happened to Edith.

"He's having a private word with his solicitor. This is great, Jude, thank you, but I wish we had proof that he killed Joe Collins."

"Sure it was him?" Jude said.

"All my instincts say so, plus it's Ronzo that Lee is afraid of. He may come across as a bit of a joker in the hot seat, but that's an act. That young man is a malicious killer who doesn't give a damn who he hurts. Getting him for the kidnaps is just the start."

"We have Joe's body and belongings," Jude said. "Give me a little longer and I'll see what else I can find."

* * *

Rachel and Elwyn returned to the interview room. There was an atmosphere — Ronzo and Fortune had been arguing.

"My client wants to talk about a deal," Fortune said. "In return for immunity from prosecution, getting him to a place of safety and a new identity, he'll tell you who is behind it all, who wanted the kidnaps carried out and what he knows about the murder of Brendan Blackmore."

Fortune did not look happy about this. "Are you all right, Mr Fortune? You look a bit put out by your client's decision."

"It's his choice."

"What about the murder of Joe Collins? Do you know anything about that?" Rachel asked Ronzo.

"Neither of those killings was down to me," Ronzo said.

"I suspect you are working with at least one other person. You kidnapped James Agnew, but it wasn't you who left him at the health centre. Want to give me his name?" Rachel said.

"No comment."

"Okay, this is what we'll do. First you will give me your real address so we can carry out our search."

Ronzo didn't appear bothered. "Pass us a pen and paper."

Watching him write it down, Rachel wondered why he hadn't just come clean in the first place. "You still have plenty of questions to answer, Ronzo, before we talk about a deal. When you took the baby and Edith, who did you hand them over to?"

That threw him. Ronzo hesitated, as if he wasn't sure what to say. "Just a man. I didn't know him, so no use asking."

"Young? Old? Tall? Fair or dark? Come on, Ronzo, you can do better than that. A description for starters," Rachel said.

"I can't remember. Tall, but I didn't see his face. He wore a balaclava whenever we met."

Just like the man at the health centre. For now, Rachel gave him the benefit of the doubt. "Right now there are forensic scientists poring over Joe's body and belongings. The same is happening with Blackmore. If they don't find anything to incriminate you, we can talk again about the possibility of a deal."

Ronzo nudged Fortune and grinned. "Nice one. Do I have to stay here while I wait?"

"Yes," Rachel said. "You will remain in custody until our investigations are complete."

Rachel picked up the file and the paper with the address on it and she and Elwyn left the room. "He's up to something but I'm damned if I can work out what."

"All that today, sending us to that apartment — delaying tactics d'you think?"

"No, Elwyn, I think it was all part of his plan. Ronzo wanted us to find something."

"The place was pristine. There was nothing to find."

"Yes, there was. You're forgetting, Elwyn, we now know that apartment belongs to Grace Blackmore. Ask yourself, given what Lee told us, is she behind what's happening to the Trio?"

CHAPTER FORTY-TWO

Grace Blackmore was outraged at the mere suggestion that she should go to the station. The uniformed PC accompanying Kenton stood well back as she turned on him.

"I've just lost my husband," she screamed. "It was me who reported him missing. Now you have the cheek to question me about his murder."

"Just come down to the station, Grace, and answer a few questions. It'll be easier if you're not here while we search."

"Search? What search? What are you expecting to find?"

"It's just routine, Grace. A few hours and it'll all be over."

"I can answer questions perfectly well here."

"Ring a solicitor if you want one. Tell him to meet you at East Manchester station."

Those dark eyes of hers narrowed in anger. "You're a disgrace, Kenton, d'you know that? And this won't go unreported. I'll be on the phone to the ACC the minute I get home."

He shrugged. "Your prerogative."

The PC led the way out to the police car and helped Grace into the back seat. Kenton, waiting at the house for the warrant and the search team, watched them drive off.

He knew the others could be some time. Time he could make use of. He walked around the garden checking the layout. Brendan Blackmore had been held somewhere, why not here? The place was large enough. There was a stone outbuilding, a greenhouse and a wooden tool-shed. He tried the doors, all were open except the shed which was locked.

One hefty shove with his shoulder and the door gave way. Inside, the place was neat and tidy, not a thing out of place. A large bench occupied the centre and tools of all kinds hung in rows on the walls. The cupboards had all the contents labelled. Whoever used this place was meticulously tidy.

After a quick glance around, Kenton's attention was taken by an old dining chair in the far corner. It was out of place, lying on its side and with a broken leg. Hanging from the back was a strip of gaffer tape that had been cut, some of it was strewn on the floor. Kenton took a closer look. The wall here was painted black and there were deep rents in the surface, as if someone had banged and scratched at it in an effort to attract attention.

Kenton heard cars pull up in the drive outside and went out to meet them. "Rachel," he called out. "Grace is on her way to the station. Have you got the warrant?"

"Yes. Where d'you want us to start?"

"The outbuildings first," he said. "I've found something interesting in the tool-shed."

* * *

Within the hour, they had a full forensic team at the Blackmore house. The evidence Kenton had stumbled on was significant.

"Jude is certain that someone was held in there," Rachel told Kenton. "Until she's done tests, she can't say for certain that it was Brendan Blackmore. But if the paint under his nails is a match for what's on the walls in that shed, then we can safely say this is where Brendan was kept in the days leading up to his murder."

"Why, Rachel? Why kidnap your own husband, hold him prisoner and then kill him?"

"We don't know that Grace did kill him, sir. This might be her property, but she may have known nothing about it. On the other hand, if she was indeed taking over the Trio, then Brendan would have information she'd need. You heard what Ronzo said about the way they operate. Each with their own piece of the pie and none of the others knowing the details."

"They don't trust each other. Can't say I'm surprised if this is what they're capable of."

Jude came out of the shed, removed the hood of her forensic suit and her mask and joined them. "If it was Blackmore in there, he tried damned hard to get out. Those scratches go deep into the wood. He must have been in there a while. From what I have seen so far, I'd say he was taped to the chair with his back to that far wall. He could just about reach it with his fingers. The poor man must have been desperate, to tear at it like that."

"We've found nothing of interest in the house, sir," Elwyn said, joining them. "There's a ton of paperwork in the office but most of it has to do with the development company they run."

"Thanks, Jude," Rachel said. "We'll leave you to it."

Kenton took off back to his car. Rachel waited until he was out of earshot before she confided in Elwyn. "It's shocking that Grace could do this to her husband but in many ways it's a relief. At least now I know this entire thing has nothing to do with Jed."

"You didn't really think it did, surely?"

"It sounds terrible, Elwyn, but I couldn't make up my mind."

Kenton unlocked his car, turned back and called to Rachel. "We should return to the station and see what Grace has to say for herself. I'd like you to sit in. This is one interview I'm not looking forward to."

CHAPTER FORTY-THREE

It was late afternoon by the time Rachel and Elwyn got back to the station. Rachel went straight up to the main office to grab a coffee before the interview.

"D'you think she's really capable of killing her husband?" Elwyn asked. "They've known each other since they were teenagers. She didn't just kill him either. Look at the hell she put him though."

"Don't be taken in, Elwyn. That woman is hard and calculating. I wouldn't put anything past her. Brendan Blackmore was nominally a member of the Trio but for all we know Grace could have been pulling his strings and finally decided she wanted it all for herself."

Interesting as it was discussing the whys and wherefores of Grace's actions, she didn't have long. Kenton would want to get this started soon. She disappeared into her office to ring home. There was no reply. By rights Jed should be getting tea for the kids about now, so what had gone wrong? She rang Mia's mobile — engaged. She'd be chatting to Chloe. Well, she couldn't worry about that now, Kenton would be waiting for her. As she left the main office, she had a quick word with Elwyn. "If Jed or Mia rings, tell them I'll be late."

Out in the corridor, Rachel took a deep breath. The prospect of interviewing Grace Blackmore scared her. This woman was both powerful and evil, not someone you crossed lightly. She held grudges, maintained she always got her own back on anyone who went against her. Grace knew who Rachel was, knew she lived with Jed McAteer and had a family. This was one of the rare times in her life when she felt vulnerable.

Kenton didn't look happy about the impending interview either. When Rachel entered his office, he was pacing the floor, a frown on his face.

"We'll make a start, but until we have the forensics it's tricky. That solicitor Grace has employed is top notch. If she doesn't talk, tell us about her part in this, he'll have her out within the hour."

Rachel shuddered. "In that case we're stuffed. How likely is it that Grace will tell us anything useful at first interview? We've humiliated her, dragged her down to the station, taken prints and DNA. She gets out, we'll be lucky to live through the next twenty-four hours."

A little over the top, but Rachel could see from his face that Kenton got the message. "I'll lead," he decided. "If things get hairy, you play the good guy."

"Grace will see right through that one, she's not stupid."

* * *

Rachel and Kenton entered the interview room and sat at the table opposite Grace and her solicitor. Immediately Grace fixed her dark, expressionless eyes on Rachel.

"You are making one huge mistake, lady. I won't forget this, the distress you've put me through."

The solicitor cleared his throat. Rachel took that to be a gentle warning for Grace to watch it. He didn't want her making any threats. He was a partner in a firm of solicitors with offices in Spinningfields. They specialised in high-end cases that earned money, no legal aid clients for them.

He certainly looked the business — the expensive suit and gold Rolex. Rachel looked at the name in the file — Gareth Gemmell. She wondered if Jed knew him, if he'd ever done any work for his firm.

"Tell me about the wooden tool-shed in your garden," Kenton began.

"No comment."

Rachel groaned inwardly. If Grace kept this up they'd get nowhere, and it'd be a long night.

"Surely you knew what was going on in there," Rachel said. "After all, Grace, it's your shed and it's in your garden."

"That shed is in a far-flung corner of my garden. My garden is large and has a shrubbery that hides all the out-buildings from the house. There is a gate only a metre away from it that leads onto a narrow lane at the back. Anything could happen up there after dark and I'd be none the wiser."

"That's where Brendan was held, wasn't it?" Kenton said. "Taped to a chair for days on end and so desperate he clawed at the wooden wall behind him in an effort to free himself."

Grace glared back at him. "I had no idea and as I've just explained, no way of knowing. D'you imagine that I'd do that to my husband? You're deluded, Kenton, and you'll pay for this, you both will. I'm not the sort of woman who forgets in a hurry." She turned her black eyes Rachel's way. "Mac has a lot to answer for. He will rue this day. And not only him, you and that family of yours too."

Gemmell whispered something in Grace's ear. Rachel could see from his face that he wasn't happy with this. Grace might have the money to pay for his services, but she was volatile, a huge risk to his firm's reputation.

"I'd like a word with my client," he said.

"Make it quick," Kenton said. "We've a lot to get through."

The two detectives left the room. Rachel was shaking. Grace Blackmore unnerved her. "We're getting nowhere," she told Kenton. "She's never going to admit to harming Brendan, no matter how long we keep her here."

"I tend to agree. Outrage and threats apart, what d'you think? Did she kill him or not?"

"Keeping him prisoner in that shed is one thing, but she'd need help to move and dump him. There's the beating too. I don't see that being down to Grace."

"Ronzo?"

"Possibly. He doesn't come across as a hardened killer but he's clever."

"Let's have another word with him before we return to Grace. If he knows she's here, in the same situation as him, it might loosen his tongue," Kenton said.

"We should ask him again about the kidnaps. We need to find Edith Hutton."

"When we're done, get onto our media people and ask them to put a photo of Edith Hutton out there," Kenton said. "With the woman's image on the news we might get a response. You never know, someone might have seen something."

CHAPTER FORTY-FOUR

Kenton smiled at the young man seated in front of him. "It's time to talk about that deal you're so keen on, Ronzo."

"You got proof of my innocence then?"

"No, quite the opposite. You're as guilty as sin, but that doesn't mean we can't discuss parameters," Kenton said.

Ronzo shook his head. "You want me to talk. I do that, I get shafted when your people come up with evidence to throw my way."

Kenton gave him another smile. "If what you tell us proves useful and we get a conviction, the CPS may be willing to look at your case leniently. Of course, you'll still have to testify in court."

Ronzo turned to look at his solicitor. Nigel Fortune was shaking his head.

"No way," Ronzo said. "I give evidence in court and that Blackmore bitch will have me killed. I tell you what I know and disappear. I'm not agreeing to owt else."

Rachel looked through the statement he'd given earlier. "Previously you referred to the boss as 'she,' but now all of a sudden, she has a name. Want to explain?"

Ronzo shrugged. "The address I gave is her apartment, you know that, so what's the difference?"

Rachel was watching Fortune. He had to mean Grace Blackmore but now he didn't seem bothered by Ronzo's slip-up.

"You're telling us that Grace Blackmore is behind the attempt to take over from the Trio?"

"If I admit it, say as much for the tape, she'll kill me."

"Just tell us, Ronzo," Rachel insisted.

A quick look at Fortune, who gave him a nod, and Ronzo said, "Grace Blackmore planned the lot. She wants what the Trio have for herself."

Now they were getting somewhere.

"You've done the right thing," Kenton said. "We have Grace Blackmore here in custody. She can't harm you."

"She's here, banged up like me?" The idea seemed to amuse him, and he broke into a wide grin. "D'you hear that? The old bat's on her own, locked up at last. Got nowt to lose in that case, have I?" Fortune gave him another nod. "It was Grace Blackmore hired me to kidnap the kid and the old woman."

"Do you know what happened to them?" Kenton asked.

"Nah. All that interested me was the money. She sorted the details, the nursery, the uniforms and that. All I had to do was find someone to act the part of the babysitter."

"Lee."

"Yeah. She didn't take much persuading. She reckons the Trio killed her sister. Lee wanted revenge so bad she'd have done anything."

"So, what did Grace intend with the kidnappings? What did she hope to achieve?" Kenton asked.

"They were leverage to persuade her partners to tell her about their side of the operation."

"Thanks, Ronzo," Kenton said. "Just what we need. You'll remain with us for the time being for your own safety. Plus we'll have a few more questions."

* * *

"Do we tackle Grace again?" Rachel asked as the door closed behind them.

"I'm going to make her wait. She can spend a night in the cells, and we'll interview her again in the morning, face her with what Ronzo told us."

"She won't like it."

"She has no choice, Rachel. We now have a witness who's told us she organised the kidnappings. Speak to Jude, we need any evidence she can find and urgently. When we face Grace tomorrow, I don't want her to have any way out."

"Someone should tell her she's staying. That solicitor of hers will try to get her out of it."

"We've got Ronzo's statement. He's named her, and that'll do for me."

By now all Rachel wanted to do was get off home, but the duty sergeant had left a message on her desk. Ray Hutton was downstairs, asking for her. She'd no idea what he might want, hopefully just an update on his mother.

Grabbing her things, she went down to meet him. A quick word and then she'd be off home.

"This is driving me mad," he said as soon as he spotted her. "You have to find her soon. Please, you must bring my mother home."

There was real pain on his face, and Rachel felt a stab of guilt. They hadn't put their all into finding Edith, and that could have repercussions for the old lady. It wasn't that the team had been slacking, it was the pressure of everything else. "We're doing our best, Mr Hutton. We're about to release her picture to the newspapers and the TV stations. By morning everyone will be aware that she's missing and what she looks like."

"No, you mustn't do that," he snapped. "If she's still alive there's a chance the kidnapper will decide he can't risk letting her live. Her face all over the media will be my mother's death warrant."

"We think it will help us to find her, Mr Hutton."

"Well, it won't, it'll make things worse."

He was angry and Rachel couldn't blame him. They should have moved on this days ago.

"I'll level with you," he said. "I know you've arrested someone. Well, that someone knows a lot more than he's telling you."

Rachel was taken aback. She presumed he was talking about Ronzo, but how did he know? "I can't discuss that with you. But, yes, we do have someone in custody."

"Look, love, solicitors talk to each other. That crook Fortune the lad's got working for him has a loose tongue. I don't know what his game is, but he made sure Gemmell knew about the young man you're holding."

"I still can't discuss it," Rachel said.

"Well, I'll tell you something I bet he's not divulged. That little thug has been working for Grace Blackmore up at the house — doing odd jobs, a little gardening, that kind of thing. She's had him around these last twelve months or more. Think on that, the pair know each other so it's anyone's guess what they cooked up between them. Brendan was my friend, Grace too, but recently the pair have been at loggerheads. You know about the young woman Brendan was seeing?"

Rachel nodded. "I've spoken to her."

"I bet she didn't tell you that Brendan planned to leave Grace for her, and that he'd even bought a house for the pair of them in Cheshire. Grace's days at Brendan's right hand were numbered, I'm afraid."

Rachel said nothing to this, but Hutton's account of the affair was a long way from what Caroline Jones had told her.

He brought his face close to Rachel and hissed, "Them two know where my mother is. So make them talk while you've got them here. Anything happens to her and I'm holding you responsible." He backed off a little. "Do your damn job for god's sake."

CHAPTER FORTY-FIVE

Day Seven: Saturday

It being her first weekend after going back to work, Rachel had hoped to spend it at home with the family, but given the pressure the team were under there was no chance of that. Kenton had the itinerary planned, and most of it involved Grace Blackmore. That meant a fun day with the woman alternating between throwing a strop and lying through her teeth. There was no way she was going to admit to anything, so Rachel could only hope that whatever Jude turned up in the way of forensic evidence was robust enough to convince the CPS they had a case that would stand up in court.

A peck on the cheek for Jed and a cuddle with Len and she was off. Mia had stayed over at Chloe's and wouldn't be back until later.

Given it was a Saturday, the roads were quieter than normal. Pulling into the car park, she could see that Kenton and Elwyn were already here but there was no sign of Amy. Jonny had got himself a flat off Chorlton Street in the city, so he usually walked in.

Last night Rachel had rung Kenton and told him about her conversation with Hutton. He'd agreed that they should re-interview Ronzo this morning. He'd also told her to go ahead and inform the media. In Kenton's opinion, it was a risk worth taking.

"The duty sergeant told me that Blackmore hasn't slept," Elwyn told her. "Apparently, she complained all night, screaming and shouting, mostly about the mattress she had to lie on and the food."

"Well, we're not a hotel," Rachel said. "Has anyone spoken to Jude?"

"She'll ring you shortly," Elwyn said.

"Rachel." Kenton was standing in the doorway. "We should have a chat before we start."

"Your office?"

"Bring the file on Leona Lomax."

Rachel grabbed the file, which was lying on her desk, and followed in Kenton's wake.

"We need to find that young woman and bring her in. She could have vital information about the case. We have no suspect for the Joe Collins murder and in case Jude doesn't find any forensics, Lomax can tell us who he knew, where he went."

Rachel had her doubts about them finding her. It was a big city, the streets were her natural environment and she could be anywhere.

"We've put out a call for her, but I doubt it'll bear fruit. As for Joe, Jude is still working on the forensics. She may come up with something that puts Ronzo in the frame for his murder." Rachel still felt bad about allowing Lee to do a runner. Change of subject. "If we don't get anything on Blackmore today, Gemmell will insist we let her go."

"The chances of her admitting to anything are slim. It's how she is, how she's always been. Deny the lot and leave finding proof she did do it to us."

"Fair enough, that's her prerogative, but if there is anything, sir, Jude will find it. She's the best in the business."

"I am going to delay the interview with Blackmore until Jude contacts us. At least we'll know what we're up against then."

It was all they could do. "Want another crack at Ronzo while we wait?" she said. "We've got Hutton's information to face him with."

"I'll have him brought up."

* * *

Nigel Fortune wasn't happy at being called out on a Saturday. "My client has shown his willingness to cooperate, what more d'you want from him?"

"The truth," Kenton said.

"You didn't tell us you worked at the Blackmore house," Rachel said.

"So? Nowt wrong in that," Ronzo said.

"Is that when Grace told you what she had planned?" Kenton asked. "Only, to me, you don't seem the type she usually trusts."

"I told you, I worked with her on the takeover. I'm a useful guy to have around." He grinned.

"Tell us how you ended up doing Grace's dirty work, Ronzo. How did she broach the kidnaps with you?" Kenton asked.

"Before I knew what she was really up to, I worked up at her house for a while, doing odd jobs and the like. She caught me with some dope. Not much, just a bit for my own use. She thought I'd stolen it from a visitor of hers, but I hadn't. We got talking, and she realised I could be useful as more than just a handyman."

"Did you know she had her husband imprisoned in the garden shed?" Kenton asked.

"Yeah. She said it was to soften him up. She needed him to talk, tell her about his part in the Trio's operations but he was stubborn. I took him the odd drink and bite of food. I didn't like what she was doing, but it were none of my business."

"Did you help to kill Brendan?" Kenton asked.

"No. I wasn't part of that. Not long before the kidnaps, I turned up for work one day and he was gone. She wouldn't tell me where, just that he wouldn't be a problem anymore."

"What did you take that to mean, Ronzo?" Rachel asked.

"That she'd had him sorted — you know. Killed."

"And that didn't bother you?" she asked.

"I thought it was best to keep out of it. She's got a real temper when she's crossed. She never spoke about her husband again and neither did I."

CHAPTER FORTY-SIX

Interview with Ronzo over, Rachel returned to her office just in time to take a call from Jude.

"Good news and bad," she began. "When we searched the Blackmore house we found a revolver, but it wasn't the gun used to shoot Brendan. The bullet we retrieved from the dump site came from a Glock."

"No other weapons?" Rachel asked.

"No more guns. We have the lump hammer used to beat him and the tape that secured him to the chair. Both have Grace's prints on them, and DNA tests confirm that Brendan was tied to it. The paint under his fingernails is the same as that on the shed walls."

"Anyone else's prints or DNA?" Rachel asked.

"No, and that bothers me. Someone strong delivered the beating, it was ferocious and sustained."

"Grace has a temper all right but she's a woman in her fifties," Rachel said. "I'm not sure she is physically capable of doing what you describe."

"Perhaps she didn't, Rachel, but someone wants you to think she did. Someone has made a pretty good job of cleaning the shed, but we have found traces of Brendan's blood on the floor. Given we can find no evidence of blood splatter on the walls or floor, and the PM results we know he wasn't killed there."

"Beaten and carted off via that back gate in the garden to Jed's site and killed there. At night, under cover of darkness no one from the house would see or hear anything."

"We intend to revisit the site, but it's a bit of a mess. It is a building site after all. Brendan was shot in the head at close range. Whoever did that would have a large amount of gunshot residue on their clothing. Find that clothing and I'll give you your killer."

Rachel closed her eyes, mentally going through all the places they'd searched. The Blackmore house and outbuildings certainly, the apartment belonging to Grace, and Ronzo's tiny flat in Longsight. "Have you got anything that points to Grace specifically?"

"Apart from the prints on the hammer and the tape, nothing."

"The fact that Brendan was held in his own garden shed is circumstantial. Grace maintains she had no idea he was there and who's to say she's not telling the truth? A barrister could argue that she could have used anything in that shed at any time in the past. We only have Ronzo's word for it that she's involved at all."

"I would suggest that you question what Ronzo told you and why he might lie about Grace being involved."

"We will, and thanks, Jude."

It was a huge disappointment. There was no chance of them holding onto Grace now. It was perfectly reasonable for her prints to be on anything in that shed — after all, she owned the house, and could have handled anything in it or the outbuildings. It was the word of a known dealer against that of Grace Blackmore, supposedly a pillar of the community. The CPS would never wear it.

Time to tell Kenton. He'd hit the roof. He was counting on Jude finding just the piece of the puzzle they needed to throw the book at Grace.

A despondent Rachel went out into the main office to tell the team. They were gathered around Jonny, who was on the phone.

"We've had a call from a woman in Blackpool. She reckons Edith Hutton is with her," Elwyn told her.

"Was that down to the media?"

"Yes. She saw Edith's photo on the news this morning and rang in straight away."

Jonny finished the call and handed Rachel a name and address. "Her name is Betty Cullen. She's a nurse and was hired by Ray Hutton to take care of his mother for a couple of weeks. The hotel in Blackpool was booked for the duration."

"Is she sure it was Hutton who hired her?" Rachel was confused. Ray Hutton, Edith's own son? Okay, he was a member of the Trio but still.

"She gave us his name, ma'am."

"Are they still there?" Rachel asked

"No," Jonny said. "Betty Cullen got an angry phone call from Hutton this morning that got her frightened. The pair of them are waiting for us in a café on the front."

Hutton had been against the media getting hold of Edith's disappearance and now Rachel understood why. "Ring Betty Cullen back, tell her we'll get the local force to pick them up. We'll send someone from here to bring them home. Tell her not to speak to Hutton again. Once they're back we'll find them a safe address until we get this sorted."

Rachel looked around the room. Her eyes settled on two uniforms. "Take a drive to Blackpool nick, bring the two women back here until we have an alternative place ready."

"What is Hutton up to?" Elwyn asked, looking at the incident board.

"I don't know but we'll alert the Blackpool force and put out a call for his arrest. While we wait, we'll pay a visit to his address and see what we can find."

"It looks like he kidnapped his own mother," Elwyn said. "If I'm right, you know what that means?"

"Yes, Elwyn. We've been wasting our time. Grace could be telling the truth after all." She looked at Jonny. "But just in case, check something for me. Find out if Brendan or Caroline Jones were about to buy a house in Cheshire. If it turns out to be true, get the details."

Rachel went to tell Kenton. He was expecting her to join him for the interview, but this would change things.

"We should ask her about Hutton, sir," Rachel suggested. "She knows him far better than us."

He had Jude's preliminary report in his hand. "We've got precious little on Grace other than forensics, which can be explained away, and the word of a budding gangster. I'm going to delay doing anything about her until we know what Hutton's been up to. But if he moves into prime suspect position, we won't have any choice but to release her. As for speaking to her about Hutton, I doubt she'll want to help us with anything. She already considers that we've treated her appallingly."

"That can't be helped. Until now Grace was all we had, which is down to Ronzo. That young man needs re-interviewing. He's done nothing but spout a pack of lies from the moment he was brought in here."

"When Hutton's brought in, Rachel, you speak to him. Even with this turn of events, we still don't have any evidence to help us find who killed Joe Collins and Brendan Blackmore."

CHAPTER FORTY-SEVEN

Since it was a weekend, Kenton made special arrangements with a magistrate he knew to get the search warrant. Within the hour, Rachel and Elwyn pulled up on the road outside Hutton's house with a police car and two uniformed officers behind them. Hutton's car wasn't on the drive and all the blinds were closed.

"Not up yet?" Elwyn suggested.

"I'll lay odds he's on his way to that hotel in Blackpool to get his mother." She looked at the front door and rang the bell several times with no result. She turned to the officer carrying the battering ram. "Get us in."

Inside, the place was neat enough, though they saw indications that Hutton had left in a hurry. There were breakfast pots on the kitchen table and upstairs the bed was unmade and strewn with clothes.

"He saw the appeal for his mother on the morning news and left straight away," Rachel said. "Now I know why he didn't want me to tell the media about Edith being missing."

"You've got him down for this, haven't you?" Elwyn said.

Rachel nodded. "I have now. Ronald Wade — Ronzo — has fed us a pack of lies. He must be under orders from Hutton."

"There is evidence. What about Grace's prints on the weapons in the shed?"

"Simple enough to fix, use some pretence, hand Grace the hammer, take it back and her prints are all over it. That must have been done by Ronzo and placed for us to find. I'll start up here in the bedroom and check for the dark clothing Jude spoke to me about. Elwyn, you look for the Glock."

Rachel put on a pair of nitrile gloves and began to search. It didn't take long. At the bottom of the wardrobe and pushed to the back was a carrier bag. She emptied the contents onto the bed and found a pair of trousers, a hoodie, and a balaclava, all black. It looked as if they'd found the man on the CCTV footage from the health centre. Balaclava man.

She needed to get these to Jude quickly so she could examine them for gunshot residue. "Elwyn," she shouted, taking the stairs. "I've found some clothing hidden up here, all black, and there's a balaclava too."

Elwyn matched her find with one of his own, a Glock revolver. "Look what I've turned up."

"Where?"

"Wrapped in plastic and stashed in the downstairs toilet cistern along with the ammo. Not very original."

"You're forgetting, Elwyn. Hutton is one of the Trio. He isn't used to doing his own dirty work. The takeover is such a big deal and so hush-hush he obviously couldn't trust anyone else. The inept way he's hidden valuable evidence shows just how out of practice he is." Rachel looked around the room and spoke to one of the uniforms. "I want this place sealing off and a full search team and Forensics in here. We'll go and see Jude, hand over what we've found."

"Are you okay? You've gone pale," Elwyn said.

"I'm shocked, to be honest. I didn't suspect Hutton. He was always in the background — the man with the missing mother who up until yesterday hadn't made much of a fuss. But that was an act. This entire thing, the takeover, the kidnappings and the murders are down to him. The evidence we've gathered here will hopefully prove he killed Brendan.

What we need now is the evidence to help us find who killed Joe Collins."

* * *

Clothing and Glock delivered, Rachel and Elwyn returned to the station.

"Fancy some breakfast?" Elwyn said. "It's a weekend, we deserve to splash out."

"I couldn't eat a thing," she said. "Coffee, yes, but it'll have to be upstairs. I should tell Kenton about the search. The poor man will have a lot of grovelling to do when Grace finds out we made a mistake."

Rachel left Elwyn to his fry-up and made her way to the main office. Jonny had the information she'd asked for.

"Neither Brendan Blackmore nor his lady friend were in negotiations to buy a house," he said.

"A lie then. I think it's about time we spoke to Ronzo again. Although I don't know why, he hasn't uttered a word of truth since we brought him in."

"Kenton's around, he's asking if you're back."

Rachel took a deep breath. "Better give him the news then. Whether he'll see it as good or bad is debatable." She shook her head. "We've both made a very real and powerful enemy in Grace. She'll want to get even with Hutton for killing her husband but she won't forget what we've put her through either."

CHAPTER FORTY-EIGHT

"Our young friend Ronzo first and then we'll tackle Grace," Kenton decided. "Have you put a call out for Hutton?"

"Yes, sir, I left that with Jonny while we searched his home. We suspect he's on his way to the hotel where his mother was staying. The Blackpool police have a full description, so it won't be long before he's caught."

"And you're sure you've got the right one this time—?" Rachel nodded — "fair enough." He sighed. "And then we start all over again."

"This time we should have the forensic evidence we need. Jude is working on it now. She has the gun we reckon killed Brendan and the clothing we suspect the killer wore."

"It's the 'suspect' and 'reckons' that bother me, Rachel. The case needs an injection of certainty. We need hard evidence, then I might sleep nights."

The pair made their way to the interview room to speak to Ronzo. Fortune was in the corridor, checking his mobile. He looked anxious.

"I'd like to get this started as soon as. I have to be somewhere else this morning," he said.

"We're as eager to finish this as you are. It'd help if your client told us the truth," Kenton said.

"He's expecting to broker a deal. I hope you have something to offer him."

Kenton chose not to answer. Instead, he said, "I've requested that he be brought up." At that moment, his mobile rang, and he walked off to take the call.

"I hope there's not a problem," Fortune said while they waited. "I did request time with my client before the interview but I'm still waiting."

"They'll be up soon," Rachel said.

Rachel heard Kenton swear, pocket his mobile and then dash off in the direction of the stairs. She turned to Fortune. "Perhaps you'd like to take a seat in the interview room. I'm not sure what's going on, but we'll try not to be too long."

Having pacified the solicitor, Rachel hurried after Kenton down the stairs and along the corridor that led to the cells. Three uniformed officers were blocking the doorway of one of them. Kenton barged between them and went inside.

Rachel heard raised voices and presumed that Ronzo was kicking off. Seconds later, Kenton emerged and joined her in the corridor.

"What's up?" she asked.

"He's dead."

Stark and to the point. Rachel shuddered, suddenly very nervous.

"He's stone cold. According to the medic, he must have died sometime in the middle of the night."

"Suicide?" Rachel asked.

"Doesn't look like it. There's nothing to suggest he took his own life. He's just lying on the bed, not a mark on him. Looks for all the world as if he's asleep."

"I'll check the CCTV."

A uniformed PC cleared his throat behind her and nodded at the camera on the wall. "Someone's covered the lens with black paint," he told her. "This one and the rest on the way down to the cells."

That was all they needed. "What do we tell Fortune?" she asked.

"The truth. No point in being coy about it. There'll have to be a full enquiry anyway."

"Given the CCTV has been deliberately put out of action, do we have to consider murder, sir?" Rachel said. "We're after Hutton, and Ronzo has to have been working for him not Grace. He'll have known things that made him dangerous."

"It has to have been an inside job. You're talking about the bent copper Nell told you about." Kenton swore. "This is all we need." Addressing the uniformed officer, he said, "I want this cell sealed off. The body must not be touched until the pathologist and the CSIs have been. You will provide me with a full list of everyone who entered his cell after mid-afternoon yesterday, what he ate and what checks were made on him during the night."

Kenton had clearly had enough. After issuing his orders, he strode off along the corridor. It was pointless talking to him, he needed time to cool down. Rachel's more pressing problem was Fortune. She had the unenviable task of informing him that his client had died while in their custody.

Fortune half rose from his chair when she went in. "Look, I have another appointment in less than an hour."

"There won't be an interview with Ronald Wade, Mr Fortune. I'm afraid he's dead."

Rachel expected an outburst, accusations of police brutality or lack of care for the vulnerable, but Fortune said nothing, accepted what she'd told him without argument. Almost as if he'd expected it.

CHAPTER FORTY-NINE

"We'll speak to Grace together," Kenton said. "And we don't say anything about the young man's death."

"We'll have to tell her something. She's going to wonder why we're doing a complete turnaround."

"Well, we'll say as little as possible. We can tell her the evidence we have against her isn't strong enough. That'll do for now. Grace will find out about Hutton soon enough."

"I'm not looking forward to the tongue lashing," Rachel admitted.

"Me neither. Hopefully she'll be so pleased at getting her freedom that she'll leave quietly."

But Kenton was wrong. When she was told all charges against her had been dropped and she was free to go, Grace launched into a tirade of abuse.

"The pair of you are totally incompetent and there will be consequences. You won't get away with what you've done to me. I told you I didn't kill Brendan. How could I? He was my husband and we'd been together a long time."

"All the evidence we had pointed to you, Grace," Kenton said quietly. "We had no choice but to bring you in."

"I was set up." She looked directly at Rachel. "Whoever is behind this — and I have my suspicions — did a bloody good job. But they won't get away with it. I intend to make them pay."

"No threats, Grace, or we'll have to think again. But if you want to share your thoughts on who might do this to you, then tell us, please," Kenton said.

Grace was still staring at Rachel. "Ask her. Look at that man she lives with for a likely contender."

Gareth Gemmell, Grace's solicitor, was hovering in the doorway with her things. He handed Grace her coat and ushered her out, along the corridor towards the main entrance.

"D'you reckon there'll be repercussions?" Rachel asked.

"No, that was just bravado. Grace will go home, lick her wounds and pick up the pieces of her organisation."

"God help us!"

* * *

Rachel returned to the main office just as Jonny was putting the office phone down. "Edith Hutton and Betty Cullen have been brought in," he told her. "They're downstairs waiting to speak to you."

"Any word on Ray?"

"Not yet."

Rachel went down to reception. The two women were sitting in a small room off to the side, drinking tea.

"That nice man gave us a full pot and some biscuits." Edith smiled. "Is my Ray coming to pick me up?"

Rachel sat down opposite the women. "Betty, how did you meet Edith?"

"I was told to pick her up at Victoria station. The man who brought her drove a silver car and had Edith's suitcase in the boot. I must say she didn't seem to know much about what was happening. She told me such a tale, something about a blonde girl who had stolen her from the home. I mean, the very idea."

Rachel smiled. "That's not a tale, I'm afraid. Edith was telling the truth. What we didn't know was that Edith's son had arranged it. We thought she'd been kidnapped and were worried for her safety."

"How very odd. Her son seemed very nice — well, at first — and I was well paid."

"Exactly what were your instructions, Betty?"

"To take Edith to the hotel in Blackpool, see that she had a nice time and to look after her." She patted the elderly woman's hand. "And that's what we did. We've been everywhere including the Tower ballroom." She turned to Edith. "We loved the dancing and the music, didn't we, dear? It was all going fine until I saw the news last night and realised something was wrong. This morning her son rang me in a dreadful state. He said he was coming to pick her up and warned me not to tell anyone where we were or that he was on his way. I didn't like his tone, he sounded threatening. So then I became concerned for Edith's safety."

"You did the right thing by contacting us, Betty. Edith will be taken back to the care home, she'll be quite safe there. We'd like you to give a statement outlining what you've just told me."

"I'm not in any danger, am I? Only Edith's been telling me stories about her gangster son and his friends."

Rachel smiled. There was no sense in frightening the woman. "It strikes me that Edith has a vivid imagination. Now, the pair of you finish your tea and one of my colleagues will take you home."

* * *

Rachel was relieved to have Edith back and unharmed. It had been an eventful morning. Just time for a mug of coffee and to gather her thoughts before Hutton was brought in.

"Both kidnap victims are back safe and well," she told the team. "That's a result by any measure. What we need now is to get the evidence to convict Hutton and find out who killed Joe Collins."

"If Hutton shot Brendan Blackmore, why not Collins too?" Elwyn asked.

"Collins was shot on the street, in the alleyway where he used to bed down for the night. I doubt Hutton would have that sort of information. Even if he did, he's more likely to pass someone like Collins onto one of his minions."

"And Blackmore?"

"I think that was more personal. They knew each other, had a working relationship. Who knows what petty jealousies that threw up over time?"

"So, you reckon Hutton for Blackmore and an unknown for Collins?" Elwyn said.

"Yes, but the odds are on that unknown being Ronzo. He knew the streets and where Collins and his mates hung out, and he also knew Lee."

"All we need now, Rachel, is proof," Elwyn said.

"The Glock and the clothing should do for Hutton but proving that Ronzo killed Collins is a different matter." Rachel glanced at the clock. It would be a while before the cause of Ronzo's death was known, and they hadn't been told if the Blackpool police had apprehended Hutton yet. "Anyone wants me I'm in my office going over the statements and reports we've got so far."

She left them to it and settled down behind her desk. There was a lot to go over and think about. Nell Hennessey had told her there was a bent copper in their midst. Given that he or she could be responsible for Ronzo's death, it was now crucial that they found this person. But where to start?

Rachel couldn't believe that the culprit was one of her team and nor could Kenton. But of course there were other CID teams working out of this station and they were all privy to each other's cases.

Over the next couple of hours, Rachel went over everything again. She was about to throw in the towel and get some lunch when her mobile rang. It was Colin Butterworth, the pathologist.

"The prisoner who died in his cell, Ronald Wade. Cause of death was a lethal overdose of insulin," he said.

"Oh? As far as I'm aware he wasn't diabetic."

"He wasn't," Butterworth said. "My theory is that it was administered while he was sleeping. We had to look hard for the injection site, but we finally found it — in his belly button would you believe."

"Are you saying that he wouldn't have known anything about it?"

"He might have winced when it was done but he'd also been given a liberal dose of diazepam. He would have fallen into a coma and never come round."

"I know it's asking a lot, but is there anything on the body to give us a clue as to who did it?"

"That's Jude's domain. She'll be in touch."

CHAPTER FIFTY

"Blackpool police have caught up with Hutton. Our men are bringing him back now," Jonny said.

"Thanks, Jonny. With luck we can get the initial interview done and go home."

Finally they were getting somewhere. Rachel rang Jude. Having Hutton in custody was all very well but they needed something concrete to face him with. "Any joy with the items we gave you from Hutton's home?"

"We're still working on it. There is definitely gunshot residue on the clothing, particularly the right sleeve of the hoodie. There's blood spatter on the front too. We're testing the bullet that killed Blackmore to see if it came from the Glock. We need a bit longer, Rachel. I want to run DNA tests on the clothing to ensure that it is Hutton's and that no one else has worn it. One thing though — as well as blood there is also vomit on the hoodie. I intend to match it against James Agnew's DNA. If that checks out, it proves he handled the infant."

It all sounded fine, it was just the time it would take. "Thanks, Jude."

Rachel went out into the main office to get more coffee. Jonny was looking intently at his mobile. "Ma'am," he called to her, "I've just received this photo. I don't know what it means but you should see it." He passed her the phone.

Rachel looked at it and gasped. The image was horrific. Joe Collins, his back against the alley wall as a man dressed in black took aim at his head with a baseball bat. Rachel enlarged the image. There was no doubt, the man assaulting Joe was Ronzo.

"Who sent you this?"

"I don't know the number, and when I rang back there was no answer."

"Can you find out who it was? Get communications on it and if you get nowhere ask your friends who help out with the street people. Someone might know the number. Whoever sent you this obviously witnessed what happened to Joe Collins and we need a word."

"I'll speak to Dora and Terry. People living on the streets trust them and they have a lot of their numbers."

"Thanks, Jonny. Any chance you can get that done today?"

He smiled at her. "I'll get off to the soup kitchen and meet Terry later tonight. If I get anything, I'll ring you."

The office phone rang. It was Kenton. "We have Hutton in custody downstairs. He's not happy, was most upset at being bundled unceremoniously into a police car and driven off. He's organising a solicitor and then we'll speak to him."

"Jude is still working on the items we gave her, sir. It may be Monday before she has the full picture for us."

"We'll still interview him. At least we can tell him what evidence we've collected and see if it loosens his tongue."

"He'll tough it out, sir. His type always does."

"Regardless of how he reacts, we're keeping him until Jude has those results for us on Monday."

"Ronzo was given an overdose of insulin," Rachel said.

"Yes, Butterworth told me. PC Darnell was on duty, and he doesn't recall anyone showing an interest."

"Did he see anyone in the corridor outside the cell?" she asked.

"Yes, two of our officers, but neither of them hung around. The prisoner was given a meal at six yesterday, after which Darnell says he appeared to be asleep."

"Who took his meal to the cells?" she asked.

"That's the problem, Rachel. No one seems to know. But it wasn't one of the canteen staff."

* * *

It was mid-afternoon by the time Hutton was ready for interview. Rachel was on her way to join Kenton and Jonny was off to the soup kitchen.

"You might as well get off, Elwyn," she said. "If I learn anything I'll give you a ring later."

Hutton's solicitor was from the same firm as Gemmell. This one was called David Hope and from the way the two men interacted, Rachel reckoned they knew each other.

"You're here, Mr Hutton, because we believe you killed Brendan Blackmore," Kenton began.

Straight to the point, and why not? Rachel reckoned they'd been going round the houses for long enough with this case. "Got anything to say?" she asked.

"Prove it."

"We intend to," Kenton said. "We have taken several items from your home, and these are now with our forensic people. The results will be with us on Monday morning. We are confident that they will show you are guilty."

"It's a set-up. A good one, I'll give the bastard that. He's thought of everything, but you've got this very wrong." He looked at Kenton and then at Rachel. "What d'you people think is going on here?"

"We believe you intended to take over the Trio's operations in this city. Run things yourself," Kenton said.

"The Trio? What're you talking about?"

"Come on, Ray, even Grace didn't insult our intelligence by pulling that one. You know what I'm getting at. The Trio of gangsters who run drugs and everything else in

Manchester. You took over after Jed McAteer went straight," Kenton said.

Hutton looked straight at Rachel and smiled. "Down to you, that was. A pretty face and Mac finally sees sense. Mind you, he was always the clever one. He could get away with it, you see, never got his hands dirty. Even you lot couldn't prove anything against him."

"We're not here to talk about McAteer," Kenton said.

"I've been set up, I've already told you. Whatever evidence you think you've found will have been placed in my house." He paused, apparently waiting for a reaction, but neither detective looked impressed. "Difficult to find, was it? This evidence? Bet it wasn't. Bet everything you found looked as if it had been hidden by an amateur."

CHAPTER FIFTY-ONE

Day Eight: Sunday

Kenton had insisted that Rachel take Sunday off. It'd been a gruelling first week back so she didn't put up a fight. She was looking forward to a family day at home. She planned to read the papers in bed while Jed made breakfast, and later she'd cook a roast dinner for them all. Megan could come if she wanted. Rachel decided to ring her when she got up.

"You seen my blue sweater?" Jed asked.

He wasn't dressed for the kitchen. He was wearing a suit and tie. "The expensive one I bought you for your birthday? No, why?"

"I thought I'd take it with me."

Those few words put paid to the family Sunday. She stared at him. Not again. "Where are you going? I was planning to spend the day together and cook a meal, or is that just me being over-optimistic?"

"Sorry, love. I did tell you about the trip last night, but I think you might have fallen asleep."

Rachel couldn't recall whether he had or not. "I had a pig of a day yesterday, so I'm sorry if I missed your news."

"I've managed to offload the land — you know, the dodgy site I was trying to build houses on."

That was good news. He'd swerved a right load of problems there. "Is that where you're going?"

"No, the legal side of the deal is all sorted. I got most of the money back, so the company is solvent again — just. But I can't leave it there. I have to get things moving again and quick. There's a tract of land for sale and the auction is today."

"On a Sunday? Are you sure?"

He smiled at her. "Quite sure, and I intend to buy it."

"Somewhere in town?"

"No, Plymouth," he said.

Rachel was nonplussed. Plymouth was some distance away and well out of Jed's comfort zone. "A long way to go to work. And a big change for you. Are you sure you'll manage? Plymouth is nothing like downtown Manchester."

"The land is cheap, the houses I build will sell and there's plenty of labour locally. I can't afford to miss it."

Rachel knew little about the property and development game, but surely there had to be something nearer home? "You've got it all worked out but is it the right decision? Plymouth, Jed. What if things go wrong? Are you going to be driving down there every other day?"

"I hope not. The land is a good deal and it'll set the firm back on its feet financially. This one detour and then it's back to home ground."

"So why d'you need your blue sweater?" she asked.

"I'll have to stay over, probably just tonight but if it's any longer I'll ring you."

"You didn't say anything about staying over last night," she said. "I'm sure I would have remembered that bit."

"You were tired, you'd had a long day. I thought it better to let you talk. You rambled on for hours about the Trio and arresting Hutton, remember?"

"We've wrapped that up now, so life will be easier." She smiled. "Shame you won't be here. I was looking forward to celebrating with the family."

"There'll be other days," he said.

Rachel lay back and watched while he gathered together some clothes and packed them into his overnight bag. "Ring me when you get there, it's a long drive."

"That's why I'm leaving early."

He leaned over and kissed her cheek. Then, for a moment that seemed to last for ever, he stared into her eyes. "Take care, Rachel. Make sure you look after yourself and the kids. Remember, no matter what happens, I do love you."

Whether it was down to a fuzzy head from too much wine the previous night or just being half asleep, the significance of those words didn't strike Rachel until later.

* * *

"He promised to take me and Chloe bowling," Mia moaned when she heard that Jed wasn't home. "Chloe'll be proper pissed off."

"Language, lady," Rachel warned. "It can't be helped. It's work, and right now Jed needs all the work he can get."

"I thought he was loaded."

"Things don't always work out in business. We shouldn't take anything for granted." Rachel was collecting clothes for the wash. "You've only worn these jeans once, what're they doing in the basket?"

"Len peed on them," Mia said.

Rachel sighed and added them to the bundle in her arms. Next stop the washing basket in her and Jed's room. There was nothing much — a couple of shirts and an old black T-shirt she'd not seen before. Rachel pulled it out. By its size it had to belong to Jed. She would have added it to the pile in her arms without a second thought but a stain down the front of it stopped her. Vomit.

Rachel let the clothes she'd been holding fall to the floor. Len was not a sicky baby. He'd done the usual bringing back a bit of milk when he was new-born but nothing since. If he'd been sick, Jed would have said something.

Her stomach was churning, the thoughts in her head running wild. Her first instinct was to burn the thing, let it go up in smoke and put it out of her mind. But she could do no such thing, much as she'd like to. Rachel went downstairs to the kitchen and put the thing in a clean plastic bag. Mia was sitting at the table eating cereal.

"Has Len been sick recently?" Rachel asked.

"No, and he eats like a pig too."

"Are you sure? Perhaps Jed gave him too much feed or something."

"Len doesn't do throwing up. You know what he's like. You keep feeding him and he'll just go on eating. He's six months old. At the rate he's going he'll be huge by the time he's one."

Now close to tears, Rachel needed help. Back in her bedroom, she rang Elwyn. "I think Jed is involved in the case," she blurted out as soon as he answered. "I've found a vomit-stained T-shirt."

"You have a baby, Rachel. Don't infants and sick go hand in hand?"

"Len's different, he's never sick. I'm worried, Elwyn. I think Jed's done a runner. He concocted some story about looking at land in Plymouth, packed a bag and left the house early this morning."

"You sure it's not your imagination running riot?"

"He said things to me, Elwyn. I didn't think about it at the time but now that I do, he sounded, well — final."

CHAPTER FIFTY-TWO

Day Nine: Monday

First thing Monday morning, Rachel took the T-shirt to Jude at the lab. She told her about her fears and asked her to check it urgently for the Agnew infant's DNA, and to keep quiet about it for now.

"I know this is breaking the rules. I shouldn't come to you direct. I should go to Kenton with my suspicions — after all Blackmore's body was found on Jed's site."

Like Elwyn, Jude was doubtful. "This is you over-wrought and overworked after having such a long break from the fray. You can't seriously think that Jed is mixed up in all this."

Was Jude speaking with the voice of reason? "I don't know what to think, but I have to know one way or the other. Please, Jude, will you help me and keep it to yourself?"

Her friend nodded. "Yes, I'll do the tests and I'll ring you later. I don't for one second think you've anything to worry about, but I'll do this for you on the understanding that if I find anything untoward, you must tell Kenton."

Rachel nodded.

"Have you heard from Jed today?"

"I've heard nothing since he left yesterday. I've tried his mobile several times, but he doesn't answer. This isn't like him, and it only adds to the worry."

"He's probably on his way back." Jude smiled. "You're going to feel a bit foolish when he turns up later today."

Rachel wanted to believe her, but she doubted she'd see Jed anytime soon. She didn't tell Jude, but before she left for work, she'd looked for his passport. They kept all of theirs together in a box in her desk. Jed's was missing, which was odd since he hadn't been abroad since his friend's wedding in Spain.

"On the good news front, we're just finalising the tests on the items you gave us from Hutton's house. I'll email the report to you within the hour," Jude said.

Rachel left the lab and drove to the station. Being Monday morning, the team were all in, including Amy, who offered no explanation for her absence on Saturday.

"I've got that information about the photo, ma'am," Jonny told her. "Dora in the soup kitchen keeps a list of all the rough sleepers who visit regularly and will give her their number. It took her a while to check through it for me. She contacted me yesterday evening with a name — Sponger."

Rachel smiled. "That's not a name, Jonny, that's his street name, what the others know him as."

"I know, but it's the only one Dora has for him. Both Dora and Terry agree that he was friendly with Joe. There is no doubt that the image was sent from his mobile."

"All we need to do now is find him, bring him in and get him to give a statement," she said.

"I kept ringing him over the weekend and got nowhere, but this morning he answered," Jonny said.

Now he really had Rachel's attention. "Will he give a statement?"

"He's agreed to meet me at the kitchen at midday."

"Good work, Jonny."

Rachel went over to the coffee machine. "How are you now?" Elwyn asked her. "You don't look right."

"Worry will do that," she whispered. "But I'm coping, which is all I can do for now. I'm waiting on Jude and then I'll know for sure."

"You're tired, Rachel. You know how you get about Jed. He's left his past well and truly behind him. If you were thinking straight, you'd see that."

Rachel smiled to herself as she stirred the coffee. She wanted to agree with what both Elwyn and Jude had said to her, but she couldn't. She kept remembering the last few words Jed had said to her as he'd left yesterday morning.

Rachel took her drink to her office. The forensics on the items collected from Hutton's house would be through anytime. After that, her and Kenton would spend the rest of day wresting the truth out of him.

* * *

Kenton, Rachel beside him, sat opposite Hutton and his solicitor in the interview room.

"The last time we spoke we told you that certain items were removed from your home during the search," Kenton began. "We now have the forensic results. We have a garment, a dark-coloured hoodie that we know from our DNA tests has only been worn by you. That hoodie has James Agnew's vomit on it, and it's covered in gunshot residue." He gave Hutton time for this to sink in. "D'you want to say anything about that?"

He chuckled. "Had your people working overtime all weekend by the sound of things. Glad you're not my boss."

Kenton ignored the comment. "We also found a Glock pistol. The bullet that entered Brendan Blackmore's skull came from that very gun."

Hutton didn't appear to be bothered by the damning evidence being put to him. He shrugged, cleared his throat and nodded. "Okay, you've proved the bullet came from the gun found in my home, but that doesn't mean I fired it."

"Yes, it does," Kenton said. "The amount of gunshot residue on the clothing proves it was fired recently and the hoodie has only been worn by you."

"Fair enough, so I fired the thing, I admit it. Doesn't mean I shot Brendan though."

Kenton was silent for a few seconds while he consulted the forensic evidence in Jude's report. Then he played his trump card. "We also found traces of Brendan Blackmore's blood on the hoodie."

The room fell silent. All eyes turned to Hutton, who, for the first time since he'd arrived at the station, looked unsure. He turned to his solicitor and whispered in his ear.

"My client would like to do a deal."

Kenton heaved a weary sigh. "So does everyone who sits in that chair. What d'you have to offer?"

"You have a bent copper in this station," Hutton said. "The force pays him one wage and I pay him another. Until recently he worked for the Trio, but when I decided to take over, he stuck with me." He looked straight at Kenton. "I can give you his name."

"You want the CPS to be lenient on the back of a name?" Kenton turned to Rachel. "Surely we can find out ourselves who this person is."

"Yes, sir. We've got people on it now."

"You're bluffing," Hutton said. "You haven't a clue."

Kenton returned the stare. "Whether we have or haven't is no concern of yours, Hutton. You will not wriggle out of this."

"Your bent copper killed that little thug who was working for me. Want to know who he is now?" Hutton said.

"Yes, we did think of that. We're not stupid. Why did you want him killed anyway?" Kenton said.

"He'd have talked. He had a loose mouth. I couldn't let that happen while there was still a chance I'd come out on top."

"Time to wrap this up," Kenton said and began to gather up his papers.

"You intend to charge my client?" the solicitor asked.

"Yes."

Hutton leaned forward, a self-satisfied look on his face. "I do have something else to offer. Want to know who I'm working with, who my partners are in this new venture?"

Now this was interesting. Ever since Hutton had been in the frame, Kenton had thought he wasn't in this alone.

"Go on then, surprise me."

"The copper's name, I shop my partners and I get that deal?" Hutton said.

"All I can promise is that I'll put it to the CPS," Kenton said. "But you tell me what you know first."

Kenton saw the odd look Hutton gave Rachel and knew immediately what was coming. "Leave us," he told her sharply. "Send DS Pryce in."

CHAPTER FIFTY-THREE

Rachel knew what her dismissal meant. Hutton had to be working with Jed. The way the man had looked at her was as good as saying it out loud. Back in her office, she grabbed her mobile and rang Jed. No answer. How could he do this to her? How could he believe he could just go back to his old ways and not cause havoc? This was her worst nightmare.

Rachel sat at her desk, head in her hands. If Jed was working with Hutton, the garment she'd given Jude earlier would prove it. But why would he be so careless as to leave it in the washing basket where she'd find it? Then she twigged. He wanted her to know. Last night, Rachel had told him about Hutton's arrest and the evidence they had against him. This morning she finds the T-shirt. He had to have left it on purpose, knowing she'd do the right thing. He had been protecting her career. He wouldn't ask her to choose, he never had. Jed knew how much her job meant to her.

Rachel sat and watched the hands on the office clock go round. Kenton and Elwyn had been talking to Hutton for ages. Finally, Elwyn stuck his head round her door.

"Kenton wants to see you in his office."

She looked at her friend, anxiety etched on her face. She wanted to ask the question but was fearful of the answer.

"Is this down to Jed?"

Elwyn nodded. "Yes. He, Hutton and Fortune have been planning the takeover for a while."

"Fortune — Ronzo's solicitor," she exclaimed. But then she thought about it. Well, why not? Jed would want someone in his corner and the pair had history. He had told her the man was dodgy and it was Fortune he'd met when Elwyn had followed him. They must have been planning this for a while, working on the details.

"The kidnaps were an attempt to make it simple, coerce Agnew and Blackmore into giving up the information they needed to continue as seamlessly as possible. But Brendan refused to play ball and things got messy."

"How did Kenton take it?"

"Well, you know what he's like. He doesn't give much away, but he doesn't blame you. In fact he's worried about your safety, you and the kids."

"Jed would never harm us."

"No, but there's others who would," Elwyn said. "Grace Blackmore is out for blood. She's issued threats already."

"Does she know about Hutton?" Rachel asked.

"Yes, she and Hutton use the same firm of solicitors. They're not supposed to share information but as you know, Grace is quite a force."

"Grace has threatened me and the kids?" Rachel said.

"Yes. Kenton reckons it's to get even with Jed."

Rachel got to her feet. "I have to go home, Elwyn, make sure they're okay."

"It's already been taken care of. All three have been picked up, taken home and are waiting for you in the care of police officers. They'll be safe until something is sorted."

"They'll be terrified. Megan might cope but Mia won't understand what's happening."

"Grace will be watched. If she makes any attempt against you or the kids she'll be arrested. Her power is gone, Rachel. We're just making sure you're all okay over the next week or so before she is dealt with."

"Jed and Fortune, eh. Why doesn't that surprise me?"

"Jed knew him, that's who he met that night I followed him to the pub. His work as a solicitor is nothing more than a cover."

"I feel so foolish for not working all this out," Rachel said. "I guess I didn't want to know."

"Jonny got a statement off Sponger by the way. He took the photo and recognised Ronzo," Elwyn said. "He wanted to get Joe away, but Ronzo was lashing out with that bat like a wild man. Sponger admitted he hadn't been brave — in fact he was terrified. He took the photo hoping it might help, and then ran off."

"Any sign of Lee?" Rachel asked.

"We had a call from a woman who reckons she saw her at Leeds station. We checked the CCTV but there's no sign of her."

"I don't think Lee has gone anywhere, Elwyn. She's hiding. The city has swallowed her up and until it spits her out again, we've no chance."

"We'll keep looking. Jonny's contacts have agreed to let him know if she turns up."

Rachel checked her mobile. Still nothing from Jed. "Better not keep Kenton waiting. I'll catch you later."

She walked out into the main office and a sea of serious faces. Rachel wanted to say something, reassure them, but she had no words. Her partner, the father of her son and the man she hoped to marry one day had let her down in the worst way.

They had all been right. Mac couldn't change. He was a villain to the core.

CHAPTER FIFTY-FOUR

Kenton had that serious look on his face, the one Rachel had come to dread, as it usually meant trouble coming her way.

"DS Pryce has told you, I imagine," he said.

"Yes. Hutton, Fortune and Jed planned to become the new Trio."

"I'm sorry, Rachel, but I have to ask, did you have any idea what Jed was up to?"

"Not a clue. I lived in a constant state of doubt about Jed, but over these last two years it faded into the background. I was beginning to believe I could drop the fear at last, and then this happens."

"Did you ever meet Fortune?" Kenton asked.

"No, although Jed did mention him. He acted as solicitor in the conveyancing of some land Jed bought recently."

"Do you know of any evidence that shows Jed was involved?" Kenton asked.

Rachel hated this, she felt like a suspect. He had to ask these things, and doubtless he'd soon want to search her home. "Yes. Yesterday I found a T-shirt in the wash basket. It had vomit on it. Knowing what I do about the Agnew kidnap, it rattled me. This morning I gave the garment to Jude and asked her to run tests. If the vomit belongs to the infant, it means Jed must have had him in his arms at some time."

That pleased Kenton, his expression lightened and he almost smiled. "Good move. I'm not going to ask what you told her about it but tell her the item is now officially evidence in this case."

"Is Hutton getting his deal, sir?"

"That isn't up to me, but I doubt the CPS will go for it. The fact that he's confessed might go well for him in court, but we have to remember he did shoot Brendan."

"Did he say if Jed was involved in that?" she asked.

"As Grace explained, access to the garden shed was simple enough, particularly after dark. They both took Brendan from the shed and put him in a portacabin on the site, which was where he was shot. Jed was there but outside at the time, weighing up where best to dump the body."

Rachel felt sick. That meant he was an accessory to murder. No wonder he'd run when she'd told him about Hutton. "Why leave Brendan's body like that? He wasn't even hidden properly."

"Hutton wanted him found, and he wanted Jed under suspicion. They may have been planning to be the new Trio, but Hutton didn't trust Jed and he wanted to frighten him. Let him know that crossing him was not a wise move."

"Jed must have been petrified when you spoke to him about it."

Kenton ignored the comment. "The bent copper is DCI Baxter by the way. Surprised me that did. I'd have staked my pension on him being straight."

Oddly enough it didn't surprise Rachel. He'd been all over this case just waiting to get in. "I'm sorry, sir," she said.

"Not your fault that Baxter's a rotten apple."

"Not for Baxter's being part of this," she said. "For having Jed in my life and not noticing what was going on long before this."

"He's a clever man, Rachel. It's not your fault, any of it. And while we're on about bent coppers, Nell has nothing to negotiate with on that score. She will be brought in and charged."

"Poor Nell, put on the spot by Grace, forced to do as she was told."

"If Nell gives evidence against Grace and her money-lending scam, there might be some leeway. Hutton also gave us certain information. He told me that Grace never gave it up. To this day she is coercing people into taking out loans they can't afford and sending in the heavy mob the first time they miss a repayment. We will gather evidence from any who'll give it, Nell too, and build a case. Grace Blackmore won't be free to threaten anyone much longer."

"What happens now?" Rachel asked.

"Until we have Grace behind bars, you and your family will be put somewhere safe."

"We could be there for some time," she said.

"You are not leaving the force, Rachel. There will be an enquiry but the outcome for you is looking favourable. This is a legitimate necessity because of the job. Your sergeant has an idea he wants to discuss with you. Hear him out, and then let me know. Meanwhile, you should go home to your children."

* * *

"Why can't I just go to uni?" Megan King asked her mother. "All this palaver because of your job. And what's happened to Jed? Why has everything gone tits-up suddenly?"

"Language, Megan," Rachel said. She was packing for an extended stay away and had no time to argue the toss. "Go down and make sure Elwyn's okay with Len."

"Why me? Mia's down there."

"Just do it, I'm up to my ears in clothes here, most of them yours, and you're not being much help."

"'Cause I don't bloody well want to go, that's why." Megan flounced out of the bedroom.

Rachel was working on automatic, stuffing things in bags without thinking and hoping for the best. Her world had been turned upside down and she had no idea what would happen next. She opened her jewellery box and looked at the contents. What to take? She took out a few sentimental pieces, including her mother's rings. She moved a tangle of necklaces to one side and then she saw it — a mobile phone. Nothing special, not top of the range, but fully charged and in working order. Jed had to have left it for her. She knew that none of them would be allowed to take their own phones because they could be traced that way. Mia would hate that, but it couldn't be helped. She'd been issued with a pay-as-you-go one so that Elwyn could keep in touch. She put both phones in her bag.

"You okay?" Elwyn asked from the doorway.

"Not really. What've you done with Len?"

"Megan's got him. You nearly ready for the off?" he asked.

"Yes." She smiled at him. "It's very kind of you, Elwyn. You're sure your mum and dad won't mind?"

"The bungalow in Rhos is empty. Now they've moved further down the coast, they want a tenant for it. You're doing them a favour really."

"Rhos on Sea. What's it like?" she asked.

"Small, quiet, not much going on. Perfect for you and the kids."

She laughed. "I am coming back, you know. You haven't got rid of me yet. Once Grace Blackmore is behind bars, that's me out of hiding."

"Have you heard from Jed?" he asked.

"No. Have you heard from Jude about the T-shirt I gave her?"

"No gunshot residue, which is good, but the vomit is James Agnew's," he said.

EPILOGUE

Two days later

It was almost summer. The sun was bright and high in the sky. Rachel, seated on a bench, took a lungful of fresh sea air and watched Mia run barefoot in the sand, her sister chasing her. Two teens behaving like kids again. It made her smile. Len was sleeping in his pushchair beside her, oblivious to the upheaval of these last few days.

Everything was easy here. There was no stress, no cases to solve, and Rachel knew that she and the kids were safe. Elwyn had been right in thinking this would be good for her. She owed him a lot. Rachel looked out at the sea and the horizon. It was tempting — a life by the coast, to wake each morning and take a stroll on the beach.

But then reality bit. The peaceful thoughts in her head were interrupted by the sound of a mobile — and it wasn't the one Kenton had given her.

It could only be Jed.

When she'd found the phone, she'd known it was only a matter of time before he rang her. Trust him to spoil her happy day.

"Sorry, Rachel. I didn't mean for any of this to happen," he said when she answered.

She could have argued the point, but why bother?

"You and the kids okay?"

"We're fine — in hiding but getting by. Where are you?"

"You know I can't tell you that."

"Why did you do it, Jed? Why ruin what we had? What possessed you to get involved, go back to your old ways?"

"It's who I am, Rachel. I know now that I can't ever change."

"You've hurt a lot of people. You can never come home. All the police forces in the UK and Europol have been alerted. It's only a matter of time before you're picked up."

"That won't happen. For a start I'm not in Europe." He chuckled. "And I'm not evil, Rachel. I didn't kill anyone, and I did make sure the Agnew kid was returned."

"Only after I told you what would happen if you didn't. As for Brendan Blackmore, you were there. You knew Hutton would kill him."

There was a silence, and for a moment Rachel thought he'd cut her off. Then he said, "Kiss the kids for me and don't be too angry."

"I'm not angry with you, Jed. I feel sorry for you and for me. I thought we were happy. Why didn't you say something?"

He avoided that one. "I can't talk for long. I'll ring you another time. Stay strong, Rachel. We will see each other again."

Then he was gone. Rachel stared down at the phone, tears running down her cheeks. The girls were coming — they mustn't see her like this. She quickly wiped them away with her hand.

This had to stop. Could she wipe Jed from her life as easily as those tears? If Rachel was to get any peace at all, she had to try. Him ringing her whenever he felt like it would just prolong the agony. It was over. There was no going back from this.

"Food?" she called to them. "There's a lovely little tea-room further up the prom."

"Do they do burgers?" Mia asked.

"They might."

Rachel watched them walk ahead of her. Seeing her chance, she took the mobile Jed had given her from her pocket, removed the sim card and threw it in a nearby bin. She'd dispose of the phone later and no one would be any the wiser.

Rachel had given Jed McAteer enough chances. There would be no more. From now on it was just her and the kids. Jed could make his own way. Whatever they'd had was in the past, their relationship the last victim of his inability to change.

THE END

Thank you for reading this book.

If you enjoyed it please leave feedback on Amazon or Goodreads, and if there is anything we missed or you have a question about, then please get in touch. We appreciate you choosing our book.

Founded in 2014 in Shoreditch, London, we at Joffe Books pride ourselves on our history of innovative publishing. We were thrilled to be shortlisted for Independent Publisher of the Year at the British Book Awards.

www.joffebooks.com

We're very grateful to eagle-eyed readers who take the time to contact us. Please send any errors you find to corrections@joffebooks.com. We'll get them fixed ASAP.